BOOK NEWS

Sign up for exclusive updates and offers at
news.jljarvis.com

THE HOLIDAY HIDEAWAY

THE HOLIDAY HIDEAWAY

A HOLIDAY HOUSE NOVEL

J.L. JARVIS

J.L. JARVIS

BOOKBINDER PRESS

THE HOLIDAY HIDEAWAY
A Holiday House Novel

ISBN 978-1-942767-21-3 (paperback)
ISBN 978-1-942767-74-9 (hardback)
ISBN 978-1-942767-20-6 (ebook)

Published by Bookbinder Press
bookbinderpress.com

CHAPTER ONE

CHLOE WALKED in and set down her bag and the rest of the mail, then she stared at the letter with a law office letterhead. She sat down and read it again. It didn't make sense. She picked up the phone and called her mother.

After reading it to her mom, Chloe asked, "Why would Aunt Eleanor leave everything to me?"

"I don't know. I suppose, if you think about it, who else did she have? Her stepson was... well, you know. They weren't ever close while she was married to his father, but after he sold her camera and jewelry to a pawnshop, things were never the same. As for me, I'm sure she knew I was fine on my own. I think it's wonderful that she left it to you. You're so much like her in so many ways. And all of her art and supplies must be a treasure trove for you. The last time I was in her studio, her brush collection alone was epic."

"Oh, it still is! The whole studio is amazing! But it's

her work that's just inspiring. She was always so encouraging. I used to love how she was always arriving home from some exotic place, and she would bring me some homemade artwork or craft from where she'd been. It opened my eyes to the world. Even though I haven't seen her since fifth or sixth grade, she's left a lasting impression."

"I've always regretted how we lost touch."

That was one way to put it. At the time, although her mother had tried to hide it, she'd been wounded by the loss. She had never said anything, but she got a distant look in her eyes whenever Chloe mentioned Aunt Eleanor's name. Chloe didn't know what had brought on the estrangement, and she'd been too young to be included in any discussion about it. It wasn't until the following Christmas, when Chloe hadn't seen her aunt for almost a year, that she'd asked if Aunt Eleanor would be there Christmas Day. Her mother had told her she wouldn't be seeing Eleanor for a long time. Even then, Chloe had understood that meant forever in adultspeak.

Now all her mother could offer was, "I never told you what happened because I didn't know. She just cut us off."

Chloe wouldn't be put off. *Did they argue? Was there any ongoing family strife?* "There had to be something."

Her mother was silent for a moment. "There must have been, but it wasn't on my side—at least not as far as I know. I wondered for years what it was, but I've had to let it go and just view her as a fond, distant memory."

"Did you try to contact her?"

Her mother hesitated. "At first. But Aunt Eleanor was an unusual person—brilliant and fiercely independent—but also private to the point of being reclusive. Once the force fields were up, they did not come down. After a few tries, I got the message." She sighed. "I think when she said, 'Please don't call me again,' I picked up on a certain reluctance."

Chloe wrinkled her nose sympathetically.

Her mother said, "She had made up her mind, so I had to respect her decision."

Chloe leaned back and exhaled. "There's something so sad about that. And so inexplicable."

Her mother sighed. "I'd seen her do it to others, but they were all friends. We were family."

"I can't imagine a life like that, closed off from family and friends."

"Eleanor knew what she wanted," her mother said. "It just wasn't us."

There was nothing more Chloe could say, but that didn't stop the nagging unanswered questions in her mind.

Her mother's voice interrupted her thoughts. "So she left you that cabin."

"Yes."

With a sigh, her mother said, "Well, you've got the winter to prepare to put it on the market in the spring, I suppose."

"Put it on the market? No. I'm going to keep it."

"But it's up there on that mountain. You'll be mauled by bears and left undiscovered until the spring thaw."

"Lovely thought, Mom." Chloe didn't bother to hide her amusement. "And since bears hibernate in the winter, any bear that attacked me would have to be rabid, so that sounds like fun."

"Well, suit yourself. At least if you start foaming at the mouth, we'll know why."

"Yup, too many lattes."

"Oh, sure, honey. You're laughing now. You're just like those animal people who say that they're just part of nature."

Chloe wrinkled her nose. "The people?"

"No, the bears."

Chloe grinned.

"But they're not part of my nature. The only nature around my house is fluffy cats and playful puppies."

"You know, Mom, they can get rabies too." Chloe shook her head. "Anyway, back to the house. Everything's in a trust. I'm supposed to call the lawyer to set up a meeting. Apparently there are some papers to sign."

Four months later, Chloe set the last box down on the counter of her new mountain cabin. "That's it. It's all over but the unpacking." She glanced about the great room, which had a vaulted ceiling, exposed beams, and a huge wall of windows facing the woods. The room was open, airy, and decorated simply to give off a sense of being surrounded by warmth and tranquility. Chloe loved it. She walked about slowly, pausing to look at items of interest. For an artist, her aunt had been amazingly organized. Chloe had always assumed other artists were like she was, right-brained and too artsy to bother with organization.

She wondered if maybe her aunt had sensed the end coming. If that were the case, she could have cleaned out the house for her own privacy as well as to spare others the burden of having to go through her accumulated clutter.

Aunt Eleanor, what was your life like all alone here? Overwhelmed by sudden sadness, Chloe got up and went out for some air.

A low hum drew her attention across the street to her neighbor's house, which looked much like hers. It must have been designed by the same person. It had the same gold-colored concrete log siding, green metal roof, and floor-to-ceiling triple-paned windows. The hum of the opening garage door stopped, and out came Paul Bunyan—at least that was who Chloe thought he looked like. Tall, broad shouldered, and wearing a plaid shirt and jeans, he strode down the driveway, dragging a trash bin on each side.

Chloe waved. "Hello!"

He regarded her for a moment then gave her a nod. It was polite enough, yet there was a distinct "leave me alone" undertone to it. He looked strapping enough to have managed a wave without straining his arm. But Chloe refused to be put off. If they were going to be neighbors up there on the mountain, far from anyone else, she would feel better if they started things off on a positive note.

With her usual optimism, she crossed the road and extended her hand. "Hi. I'm Chloe Burke."

"Luke Abbot." He shook her hand. He had a nice, firm handshake. But his hands were surprisingly soft, more like those of a guy who spent his life at a desk, not doing manly, outdoorsy things on top of a mountain.

With a weak gesture back toward her house, she said, "I'm Eleanor's niece. I've just moved in."

He frowned. "Oh. I'm sorry about your aunt."

"Thank you. So you knew her?"

"Yes."

Chloe waited, thinking he might offer more, like a nice anecdote about her aunt or a comment about what good neighbors they had been. People usually said things like that, but Luke wasn't the usual sort. "So how well did you know her?"

"Well enough." He glanced at her house then looked back toward his.

Got it. Backing off now. "Well, it was nice to meet you."

He did that chin-lifting nod thing, which, Chloe decided, was his chin's version of aloha, meant to serve as hello, goodbye, or just "Get off my lawn."

She took a step toward her house then turned back. "Oh! So today's garbage day?"

He had covered an impressive distance in a brief time, but at least he turned to answer. "No, tomorrow. I just bring my trash out the afternoon before, so I don't have to come out in the morning." He stood as if waiting to be dismissed.

Chloe smiled. "Great. So Thursday is trash day. Thanks! Bye!" She waved and headed inside before he could lift that rugged jawline with another chin nod. It was a fine, sturdy chin, but the way he nodded seemed unnecessarily standoffish to her. Maybe she'd been substitute teaching for too long. She had seen every way a middle school student could express a complete lack of interest without uttering a word, so perhaps she'd become overly tuned-in to nonverbal cues. She had no tolerance left for dismissive behavior. But her substitute art-teaching days were behind her. Thanks to Aunt Eleanor, she could start her business selling prints of her paintings along with related design products in local shops and online.

The house couldn't be more perfect for an artist. Her aunt had clearly had the log cabin customized for her painting needs, complete with a sunroom that jutted out from the side of the house with floor-to-ceiling glass walls on three sides and a two-sided fireplace that was shared with the kitchen. Custom-built cabinets, perfectly sized for an artist's needs, filled the rest of the wall. Subfloor heating kept the room toasty enough to snuggle up with a book in the overstuffed chair and ottoman by the gas-fueled fireplace.

Thank you, Aunt Eleanor. It's perfect.

CHAPTER TWO

Most people went shopping the day after Thanksgiving, but not Chloe. For Chloe, Black Friday was all red and green and always spent at home. She looked over her multiphased holiday decorating plan: a day each for outside lights, the Christmas village, her nutcracker collection, and the tree. By the end of the week after Thanksgiving, scented candles and tchotchkes would be stylishly strewn throughout the house. But that day, taking one step at a time, she would tackle the lights.

The move from apartment to house meant expanding the scope of her decorative vision, but she was prepared. She'd purchased two dozen sets of lights with sixty-seven changeable settings for eighteen hours of music-syncable LED splendor. Chloe could program them to display any color of the rainbow as well as wink, blink, or pulse against her house and its surrounding canvas of snow-dusted spruce trees. It was going to be magical.

With a playlist of her holiday favorites blasting in her wireless earbuds, she worked all afternoon, outlining the cabin in lights and using the rest of the lights to deck out the trees in her front yard. *So many lights!* She could barely contain her delight. With the finishing touches on her lighting scheme, she stood and admired her work. Phone in hand, she checked when the sun would go down then set an alarm for five minutes before sunset. She exhaled with satisfaction and went inside for a one-hour nap.

She was dozing by the fire in her overstuffed chair when her alarm went off, and she lurched upright. "Oh. Oh!" She leapt to her feet, slipped on her boots, and headed outside with the remote control for the lighting. She halted outside her front doorway. *Wow. It is so dark in the country.* She pulled out her phone, turned on the flashlight, then made her way across the road, where she would have the best view of her lighting master-piece. The remote control was a new toy that made her almost giddy with power. She was the Seurat of seasonal lighting as she pressed the on button. *Zing! Oh, the splendor!* She nodded, beaming. *Oh yeah.* The Versailles Hall of Mirrors had nothing on Chloe's Christmas lighting display.

Trying each setting on the remote, Chloe enjoyed each one more than the last, but she settled upon the elegant understatement of white lights punctuated with rhythmical blinking. Tomorrow, she would decide whether to add music. The natural pine smell from the woods all around was an unexpected bonus. This was Christmas at its best. She stood, wholly enchanted by the splendor. *Chloe, look what you've done!*

"Excuse me."

Chloe gasped and wound her arm back, ready to strike the approaching man... with her three-inch-long lighting remote.

"Whoa, it's just me. Luke. Your neighbor?"

"What the heck? You scared me!"

"Yeah, I noticed. Sorry."

"It's okay. I mean, it will be okay when my pulse settles down to two digits." She calmed down enough to study Luke's face, which was well lit by her Christmas lights. He looked harmless enough, yet history was full of people who looked harmless enough but were not. "Sorry, Luke, but I'm not good at having people sneak up on me."

He lifted a hand to his forehead as if he were shielding his eyes from the sun. "If you thought that was sneaking, you need a better radar."

"Oh, really?" That just annoyed her, even if it was true. "I'll work on it." She started back to her house as she muttered, "Bye. Have a good evening."

"Wait."

She kept walking. Should she be running instead? If he posed any threat, surely Aunt Eleanor would have warned her to be wary of him. She paused on the opposite side of the road and turned back. "Yes?"

He made a sweeping gesture toward her lights as he

tilted his head in the opposite direction. "Is this going to be a permanent thing?"

"What, the lights? No. It's just for the holidays."

"Every night?"

She heaved an impatient sigh. "Until Christmas, yes. It's kind of a tradition."

"Oh." The way he said it gave the word so much more weight than its one-syllable length implied.

She was way past sounding polite at that point. Impatience was the best she could muster. "Is there a problem?"

"Yes."

She asked glibly, "Oh, is there? What is it, Lukenezer Scrooge?"

He obviously had no appreciation for her sense of humor. He pointed at his cabin. "See that wall of windows in front? Well, that's my great room, where I spend most of my time, and your, uh, festive display is in my line of vision."

She smiled cheerily. "You're welcome."

He looked down and shook his head slightly. "What I mean is, I was wondering if that thing had a setting just a notch or two south of grand mal seizure?" His voice sounded increasingly strained.

Confused, Chloe cast a casual glance at her remote then peered at him.

His next words came out with a bark. "Could you turn off that blinking?"

His harsh tone alarmed her, and she quickly complied.

Still shielding his eyes, he winced. "Any chance there's a subtle green or red on that thing, with no blinking? Ever?"

Chloe turned the lights to green and dimmed them. "Are you okay?"

"Yeah. Sorry to spoil your fun, but the lights..." He shook his head. "I can't. It's... a health thing."

Chloe inwardly groaned. *And you had to call him a name. Lukenezer Scrooge. Way to go, Chloe.* "I'm sorry. I didn't—"

He cut her off. "It's okay. Don't worry about it." He started to leave but paused long enough to mutter his thanks before going back into his house.

CHAPTER THREE

THE NEXT MORNING, Chloe ventured down from her mountain and went into town for some groceries and assorted supplies. In addition to her decorating to-do list, she always made an effort to insert baking into the holidays whenever she found a spare hour or two. That day, she was motivated by more than just seasonal spirit. After the previous evening's incident with her lighting, she wanted to offer Luke a neighborly gesture to smooth over the tension, or rather her guilt. It had never occurred to her that flashing holiday lights could trigger whatever health episode he seemed to be suffering from. But that wasn't the worst of it. Adding insult to injury, she had called him a Scrooge.

As she struggled to recapture her Christmas buzz, Chloe returned home from her shopping and popped a package of premixed cookie dough into the oven. An hour later, she stood at Luke's door with a fresh batch of cookies in a seasonal tin.

She rang the doorbell. Orchestral music swelled and blared through the thick wooden door. She rang the bell again and knocked on the door for good measure. He certainly wasn't going to hear her over that music. She almost thought about going home and coming back later, but she decided to give it thirty seconds more before accepting defeat. She listened in hope of a quiet musical passage, but it was not forthcoming. In fact, the music just got louder. One last time, she rang the bell and knocked loudly. Just as she knocked, the music ended. Her knocking sounded more like pounding.

The door swung open. With a look of alarm, Luke asked, "Are you okay?"

Her eyes widened. "Yes, I'm fine. It was really loud. The music."

He relaxed and said, "Prokofiev." As if that explained it. "He gets that way sometimes."

Of course he does. She nodded despite having no idea what he was talking about. But none of that mattered because it was the first time she'd seen him up close in broad daylight. She wasn't prepared for his effect upon her. In an unkempt T-shirt and jeans, he no longer looked like Paul Bunyan. He simply looked rugged—not handsome or pretty—but he had a presence, an unusual quiet virility that made her suddenly realize she'd forgotten to breathe. Other men may have been as tall and broad shouldered, but Luke's aloof confidence was unnerving. She looked up, expecting to make ordinary eye contact, but the light caught his gray eyes, and it was like looking into a restless sea.

The silence was approaching a level of awkwardness she was keenly aware of yet unable to remedy. Finally, she blurted out, "Cookies." Then she grinned. "I made them. It's a peace offering for last night."

Throughout her disjointed display on his doorstep, Luke had maintained a steady gaze framed by furrowed brows. Chloe thrust the cookie tin toward him. He took it and eyed it as though he'd never seen cookies.

"They're perfectly safe. Oh, you're not a vegan, are you?" She sucked in air through clenched teeth. "I should have thought—"

"No." He chuckled at the suggestion.

"Good. And if you don't celebrate Christmas, they're just chocolate chip. You could just think of the chips as Hanukkah gelt—unwrapped, obviously. Or—"

"Christmas is fine."

She peered through doubtful eyes. "You don't sound sure."

"Sure of what?"

"Of whether you celebrate it."

"I do. I'm just pretty low-key about it."

Chloe nodded out of politeness.

He lifted the cookie tin. "But this was nice of you. Thanks."

During the long pause that followed, Chloe glanced past Luke into the large, open great room behind him. "You're so neat, just like my aunt."

"Yeah, we had that in common. A lot of things, actually. We got one another."

Chloe gave that some thought. Her seventy-something aunt and her manly thirtyish neighbor made an interesting pairing. "So, you two were close?"

He studied her for a moment. "Not like you're thinking."

"I wasn't thinking. I was just asking." She sounded defensive.

"We were there for each other when we needed to be, and we left each other alone when we didn't."

Chloe nodded as if she understood, but in the few awkward minutes she'd known him, she found herself understanding him less and less. She had a fleeting impulse to turn and make a hasty escape.

"You're not like her at all," he said.

Well, I don't "get you" like she did. Chloe wanted to smirk but suppressed it and dared to look into his direct gaze, something akin to looking into the sun. "I didn't really know her that well."

With a nod, he said, "Right. The family rift."

Chloe was taken aback but recovered. "She told you?" That went a little too far beyond idle over-the-fence chitchat.

Luke leaned against the doorframe and folded his arms. "Just that there was one. Sorry. I didn't mean to pry."

"It's not really prying if she told you about it. I just didn't realize..."

"She was alone. Sometimes talking helps."

Thank you, Doctor Phil. "Oh."

Luke's eyes softened. "I don't know the details, but I

do know that whatever happened had nothing to do with her feelings for you or your family."

Really? Something sputtered in the kitchen. She breathed in the scent, confirming the source of the sound. "I'm keeping you from your coffee."

He glanced toward the kitchen. "No." Turning back, he awkwardly asked, "Do you want some?" Without waiting for an answer, he stepped aside and started heading toward the kitchen. "You really should try this. It's from the deli in town. They roast it on-site."

Since he'd already disappeared around the corner, Chloe felt she had no choice but to follow. She took in the vaulted ceiling and beams of the great room, almost like hers. One sizable acrylic painting with a heavy Jackson Pollock influence nearly filled the largest wall, and the other wall without windows had a floor-to-ceiling stone fireplace with a built-in niche for a TV. The few pieces of furniture were substantial and comfortable looking, but each had a purpose. There was nothing extraneous. The guy was a minimalist. There was no word to describe the overall look except manly, as if a person might grow a full beard just from sitting on that massive leather sofa. She made a mental note to avoid it. Despite that, he managed to keep his facial hair to a well-trimmed stubble, dark brown with a bit of red at the chin.

Chloe sat on a stool at the island counter as Luke filled two mugs with coffee and set one before her. She blew on the top then took a sip. "Oh my gosh!"

With a knowing smile, he nodded and sat down

across from her. "Right?" He opened the cookie tin and held it out to her.

"Oh. No thanks. I might have had one or two while I packed them." *Four. Please don't count them.*

He ate one and gave her an approving nod. Pleased, Chloe studied him for a moment. She was too curious not to ask. "So, last night..."

His expression changed in an instant, and sharp eyes flicked toward her. "It's a TBI." When she failed to register a reaction, he added, "Traumatic brain injury."

"Oh! I'm sorry! What happened?"

After a brief, blank stare, he said, "I injured my brain. Traumatically."

Chloe looked away. *Wow, and I thought I made things awkward.* "Sorry. It's none of my business. I just—"

"It's okay. You don't have to worry. I won't collapse in a full-blown seizure. But if I do, just flip me onto my side and call an ambulance."

"Okay?" That didn't sound at all funny, yet he was smiling. The guy had a weird sense of humor.

He gave his head a dismissive shake. "It's more of a severe headache and dizziness situation. Oh, and occasional vomiting.

"Uh, yeah. Sounds like fun." She started to smile, but her frown won the fight.

"So if you look out the window and see me staggering blindly, you shouldn't assume it's from drinking." An unexpected grin lit his eyes. "Necessarily."

Chloe lifted her chin and nearly chuckled, but her

concern silenced it. "I've disabled the blinking, and I'll keep the Christmas lights dimmed for the duration. Let me know if they need any adjustments."

He nodded, clearly grateful, then stared into his coffee.

The ensuing silence made Chloe uncomfortable. "So, what do you do?"

"Not much."

Chloe inwardly groaned. He did not make it easy. "I mean for a living."

"The head injury knocked me out of commission, at least for the time being. But I'm an analyst."

"An analyst of what?"

"Data."

"Whose data?"

He looked into her eyes with thinly veiled annoyance. "The State Department. Before you ask what state, the US government." His mouth turned up at one corner.

"What made you think I was going to ask that?"

"Just a hunch," he said with what looked like genuine warmth.

"So... an analyst for the State Department." She mulled it over. "That's pretty broad."

"Is it? What do you do?"

"I'm an artist."

"That's pretty broad too." He looked at her differently, more appreciatively. "Are you a painter like Eleanor?"

She nodded. "Yes. I'm hoping to find a way to

monetize my art so I can actually support myself with what I do best. I don't really do anything else all that well, so that's my plan so far. Crazy, huh?"

"No, not crazy at all." He seemed to take her art aspirations seriously, which was refreshing.

She never felt comfortable talking about herself, so she changed the subject. "So what part of the State Department do you work for?"

He stared blankly. "Digital Innovation."

Chloe thought for a moment. "Like software development?"

His face brightened. "Exactly."

Moments passed while they each sipped their coffee. Luke set down his mug and broke the silence. "Well, if you need anything, you know where you can find me."

Chloe followed his lead and got up to leave. "Thanks."

"Eleanor would have wanted me to look out for you."

"Would she?" Chloe hoped that were true. Her aunt certainly had looked out for her already.

"Well, I'd better get going. That house isn't going to decorate itself." She got up, and he followed her to the door. Chloe paused. "I suppose syncing the lighting with Christmas carols is out of the question?"

He narrowed his eyes. "Yes."

She wasn't sure how to take his emphatic response. Was he angry? When he broke into a smile, she relaxed.

"There's no health reason for it," he said. "It would just be annoying."

Chloe stopped at the door. She didn't mean to squint and move closer. "Christmas carols? Annoying?"

He rolled his eyes. "Yes!"

She frowned, tried to fathom his comment, then frowned some more and leaned back. "Christmas carols." She shook her head. "Well, I was actually joking about adding music."

"I know. I wasn't." He looked at her with a wry expression she could not quite decipher.

"Oh. Okay." She tried to unwrinkle her forehead.

He opened the door then gazed down at her. "Sorry, Chloe. I'm just not the Christmassy type."

"That's okay." She tried to appear pleasant as she said goodbye, but she went back to her house feeling baffled.

All the lights and decorations weren't so much about Christmas. People had different faiths and different traditions. They were about celebrating. They made people happy. Most people. *Not Luke, evidently.*

Chloe went inside, turned on her holiday-decorating playlist, and got to work setting up her Christmas village.

CHAPTER FOUR

CHLOE OPENED THE PANTRY. Built into the door was a spice rack. "Alphabetical, of course." Chloe shook her head. "I'm not worthy." On the inside wall of the pantry was a row of a half dozen cup hooks with key rings hanging from two of them. They were labeled, naturally. One was marked "ED" for her aunt, Eleanor Dowd, and the other "LA." *Luke Abbot.* They looked like house keys. There was no other house within a half-mile radius, not to mention one owned by someone with the initials LA. She set the keys on the counter as a reminder to ask him about them, then she returned to the pantry to clean out cans of beets, sardines, and other items she wouldn't be using. When she finished, she loaded two boxes into the back of her car and headed to town to donate them.

While there, she stopped by the deli for some coffee and nearly walked past Luke as he waited in line to check out.

"Chloe?" He laughed. "Couldn't wait, could you?"

She felt a little embarrassed. "I love coffee."

"That's why I'm here. You drank the last of mine." He winked, and her heart went weightless for a fleeting moment.

With a quick look at the one bag of coffee in her basket, he asked, "Is that all you've got?"

"I went shopping yesterday, so I'm pretty well stocked."

With a conspiratorial look, he cast a look at his basket. "Put it in here. We'll settle up after."

She was going to decline the offer but then looked at the dozen people waiting behind him. He lifted his eyebrows knowingly, and she dropped the coffee into his basket. When he'd finished paying, he said, "Let's grab a cup. It's always better here than at home. You buy, and we'll call it even."

"You're not much of a negotiator, are you? I'll buy, but I'll pay for my pound of coffee."

He shook his head and frowned as though she were being silly, but he didn't make an issue of it.

They took their coffees from the counter and sat by the window amid the muted clatter and hum of the crowded shop. Chloe looked outside, where a light snow was falling. "I love the snow in December."

Luke watched the snow with her, looking as if he was remembering something. Chloe glanced over, saw his wistful expression, and chose not to interrupt his thoughts.

A tap on the window pulled her from her reverie. A

man in his twenties waved and headed inside to stand at her table. "Chloe, how are you?"

She smiled politely. "Justin, hi. I'm fine. How are you?"

"Good." He nodded and glanced at Luke.

"This is Luke. Luke, Justin."

Luke reached out, and the two men shook hands.

A sharp glint flickered in Justin's eyes, but a cordial look took its place. "Are you two enjoying the holidays?"

Luke glanced at Chloe, looking uneasy about having been lumped together, but before he could say anything, she said, "Yes, we are."

"Good. Well, happy holidays." He cast a glance at Luke, then his gaze lingered on Chloe. "Goodbye, Chloe. Nice meeting you, Luke." Then he left.

Chloe looked down at her coffee.

"He thought you and I were together," Luke said.

With a flippant shrug, Chloe said, "Well, we are. We're sitting here together, having coffee."

"You know what I mean."

"I know. Sorry. It was easier than going through a long explanation."

"A long explanation like, 'Oh, he's just my neighbor.'"

Chloe frowned and exhaled. "Okay, so I didn't want him to think I was... available."

"Glad I could be of service," he said dryly.

"I'm sorry." She really was because she felt low and deceitful.

Luke shook his head. "I feel so used."

Chloe looked up from her coffee with guilt and concern, only to see his eyes glimmer. He was joking. He always managed to catch her off guard. Feeling like he was making fun of her, she shifted from regretful to defensive. "It's just that Justin..." She looked up, searching for the best way to frame it.

Luke held up his palms. "It's okay. No need to explain."

"I just don't want you to think I treat people that way."

A smug glint came to his eyes. "Except Justin."

He was making assumptions that made her look bad, and it frustrated her. "You're right. I should have been honest and just told him our first date was so boring that I'd rather spend an evening reading actuarial tables than spend another night with him."

Clearly amused, Luke leaned back and folded his arms.

Chloe's jaw dropped. "Not that we spent the night. That came out wrong. I wouldn't spend the night with him if..."

Luke chuckled. "If he were an actuarial table?"

Chloe looked upward and grimaced. "God, I hate dating."

"Are you talking to God or to me?"

Chloe laughed. "To whoever will listen."

"I'm all ears."

Not entirely, 'cause there's a good-looking face between them. She shook her head. "There's not much more to it. I mean, how much can you tell from an app photo and profile? You take your chances and meet in real life. But five minutes into a date, you pretty much know if you'd rather be anywhere else than sitting and talking to that particular person. The rest of the evening is an exercise in patience and forced conversation. And sometimes defensive maneuvers."

"Then why do you do it?"

Is Luke nuts? "Because. It's like the lottery. You usually lose, but now and then, you get a small win. And you hear stories of people winning big, meeting their spouses online. Besides, how else can you meet people?"

He looked like he didn't believe she was serious. "In real life? At your job. In the course of a day. Look around you." He spread his hands out. "People."

She peered at him. "That's easy for you to say. I mean, look at you."

He glanced down with embarrassed confusion then back up at her with his eyebrows raised in a questioning look.

She wasn't about to feed his ego, but she felt backed into a corner. "You don't strike me as the type that has to stay home eating ramen noodles for dinner—unless you want to."

He smirked. "I live in the woods. Alone."

She gave him an impatient stare. "Oh, c'mon. If you wanted to date—"

"Actually, I can't remember ever going on a date

with a stranger." He seemed as though it were a sudden revelation.

"Which proves my point. You don't have to. If you wanted companionship, you could walk into any bar and sit down. You wouldn't last five minutes before some lovely lady joined you. Then you'd walk hand in hand into the sunset. Or parking lot."

"And you don't think you could do the same?"

She let out an unattractive snort.

Luke leaned his elbows on the table. "Have you ever tried it?"

She wrinkled her face in protest. "Why would I?"

"You haven't. You think life emanates from your phone." He looked so pleased with himself that she wanted to show him how wrong he was.

"No, I don't."

"Then prove it." A smile bloomed on his face. "Tonight."

"What?"

He nodded slowly, still smiling. "I'll be your wingman."

She leaned back, shaking her head. "No."

He continued to nod, his smile broadening. "It's happening."

"Wait. I didn't agree. And besides, I've got plans."

"No, you don't." He didn't even hesitate. He was so sure of it. "It'll be good for you."

"No, it won't. And I'm not even looking for a relationship now."

"But that's when you find them, when you least expect it."

She could not believe what he was proposing. "What's in it for you? Don't you have some fishing or bird-watching to do?"

"This isn't so different. Besides, Eleanor would have wanted me to look after you."

"When I was seven. But I'm grown up. I can take care of myself."

He nodded, unconvinced. "I'll pick you up at nine o'clock."

Her jaw dropped. By the time she shook her head, he'd already reached into his pocket, dropped a ten on the table for the coffee, and left.

"But I... I still owe you for my pound of coffee." She shut her eyes then looked out the window. Well, she couldn't just let him judge her like that. *Fine.* If it took a little humiliation to prove her point, she would do it. She would put on her big-girl pants and man up.

CHAPTER FIVE

LUKE GOT into his car and drove home, still wondering what had just happened. Had he really just made plans to go out with Chloe to prove she could meet someone without a dating app? He had never liked the idea of online dating, but this took the need to be right to a new level. It was the sort of thing he and his friends might do —challenge each other, or even bet on it, then live to regret it and laugh over beers. But he barely knew Chloe. What made him think this could turn out well? Chloe was his neighbor, not one of his friends. He had to live with her—well, not *with* her, just near her. As neighbors. That was all.

He reviewed the situation, analyzing it as though he were at work. Chloe was different. She made him think. And smile. She seemed wound up a bit tight for an artist, but it was endearing. Since he'd met her, he found himself wanting to see what she would be like if she felt more at ease, if she liked him—as a friend. Any other sort of relationship with a neighbor was asking for trouble. If things went south, he would have to face her at the mailbox, while taking out trash, or when he went jogging. She didn't strike him as a jogger. She seemed like more of a hot-yoga type.

She seemed to have no idea how interesting and attractive she was. He'd only seen her in her worn jeans and T-shirts, but he was sure that if she let her blond hair down from that ponytail it seemed to live in, she could look really hot. As a friend. What was he doing— mentally letting down her hair in a purely platonic way? Sure. Friends did that. He grimaced.

Friends. Get back on track. They were going to be friends. The truth was, he could use a friend—a real, non-work-related, easy-to-be-with friend. So why was he laying the foundation for their friendship by guiding her social life? He'd as much as taken on the role of surrogate matchmaking grandmother. It was all starting to feel very weird. He had only himself to blame. He'd had more than a few inspired, even brilliant, ideas in his time. This wasn't one of them. In fact, he would go out on a limb and call it plain stupid. He desperately hoped he was not going to regret this.

AT NINE O'CLOCK SHARP, Luke knocked on the door. For some reason that Chloe refused to admit, she was on her fifth outfit. She looked in the mirror and sighed. Well, this would have to do. She had on a white formfitting Angora sweater, black pants, and heels. She wasn't going for sexy, but she hoped to achieve a quasi-presentable impression approaching attractiveness. She rolled her eyes. *For whom? Some random guy trapped in his haircut from a decade ago who laughed while inhaling? Or maybe a guy with a file at the local precinct—Prints Charming.*

She opened the door.

"You look nice."

Don't act so surprised, and for God's sake, Chloe, do not do your Wallace and Gromit smile. "Thank you. You look nice too." *Really nice. So nice that if this were a date, I'd be looking forward to it. But it's not.*

Luke's car was parked behind hers. "Do you mind if I drive?"

"No." *But only because I hate driving.* However, that made it feel like a date. She frowned.

"Everything okay?"

Only then did she realize he'd been watching her. "Oh, yeah. I was just wondering if I left the coffeepot on."

He stopped. "Do you want to go back and check?"

"No. I didn't."

"Are you sure? We're not on a schedule here."

"No. It's fine." She resumed walking. He opened the car door for her. *Wow, this non-date is already starting out better than any real one I've been on.* She got in.

The first place they headed to was a hangout for locals. On the downside, they were locals. On the upside, they were locals. What happened in Vegas stayed in Vegas, but what happened in one's hometown stayed there forever. Chloe wanted to laugh. What did she think was going to happen, some wildly romantic encounter? With or without Luke sitting nearby and watching, nothing was going to happen. And that was the point of this whole exercise. She was not going to walk into a bar and meet the love of her life. That's what dating apps were for.

Luke parked but left the car running and turned to her. "Two seats between us at all times. Aim for the corner for better sight lines. But remember, you don't know me. If you need to be rescued, I'll call your cell. You'll pretend you have to leave, which you will, and I'll be right behind you."

"But how will you know if I need to be rescued?"

He looked at her patiently. "I'll know."

She wasn't sure she believed him. In fact, she could imagine him watching, amused, as she suffered. She could always just get up and leave, rescue phone call or not, or go the subtler route and climb out the bathroom window.

They exchanged cell numbers, then Luke said he would go in first and she should follow. As soon as he'd said it, he changed his mind. "On second thought, you go first."

"Why?" She widened her eyes. "You don't think I'll come in?"

He didn't deny it. "It's better this way." The parking lot was too dark for her to be certain, but she thought she detected a hint of a grin. "All right, Cinderella, it's go time."

She got out, took a few steps, and turned, and they nearly collided. "Let's just go get a burger. Aren't you hungry? I'm hungry."

He looked at her with a cool glint of confident condescension. "You're not scared, are you?"

"No!" She blew air through her lips. "Of course I'm not scared!" She was scared, but she wouldn't let him know that. She was so far out of her comfort zone, she could barely recall what it felt like. The last time she'd been to a bar all alone was... well, never. How had she gotten herself into this situation? Oh yeah. The bet. Was it even a bet, though? They hadn't decided on stakes. *Oh great, so even if I survive, I'll come out with nothing.* No, it wasn't a bet. It was more of a challenge. She hated competition unless it was with herself.

Chloe wrinkled her face as she drew close to the entrance. She could have been home in her comfy pants, reading a book. And who had decided the rules? Luke. He had insisted they give it three tries. *Why not two? Or just one?* Actually, she liked the way zero sounded, but no, three it was. And she had agreed to it.

The bar was packed. Chloe stood at the end of the bar. Luke walked in behind her and lingered nearby. A woman with calico hair joined him and struck up a conversation. After a few tries at getting the bartender's attention, Chloe contemplated attempting doing semaphore signals with cocktail napkins, but the bartender finally appeared, and she ordered a glass of white wine. Luke was oblivious to her present torment as he chatted it up with his new lady friend with the crazy-quilt hair.

Chloe picked up her phone and mapped out the walking route to her house. That last walk up the mountain was going to be a killer. She rearranged the apps on her phone so the rideshare app was on the first page. Then she remembered that the rideshare company didn't serve this area, so the app would be useless. She was being silly. Of course Luke would take her home if she asked him, but that would be admitting defeat. So she straightened up and decided to be tough, sip her wine, and enjoy watching Luke fend off his new lady friend's overtures. The woman was very persistent. Luke's eyes flicked toward Chloe, and she looked away, smiling.

"You look happy."

She looked up at a guy who seemed to be looking at her. "Do I?"

The man got up from his barstool. "Would you like to sit down?" He looked pleasant enough—a steady, reliable sort, probably in his late twenties.

Her eyes darted to Luke. His calico cat was still purring beside him. He gave her a nod that looked very much like he wanted to say, "Duh! Do something." So Chloe smiled and sat down. The guy offered to buy her a drink, but she lifted the one in her hand and smiled. "Thanks, but I'm good for now."

He smoothed his hair flat to his forehead a couple of

times, which must have been a habit, because it was shiny and pasted in place from the effort.

She couldn't take the silence. "So, what do you do?"

He perked up. "I'm a manager."

"Oh?" What was it with guys and occupational vagueness? First Luke "the analyst" and now this guy. *What did he say his name was? Barry. Or was it Barney? Barry/Barney, the manager.* Maybe she didn't really need to know more. But it was too quiet, so she delved deeper. No one could accuse her of not making an effort.

Unlike Luke, Barry/Barney was very forthcoming. He was a retail manager. He went on to regale her with the many facets of his daily life—rotating inventory, checking time sheets, and looking for slackers. "You can't trust people."

Chloe tried to look interested, but her mind kept straying to the mystery series she could have been binge-watching on TV. She'd stayed up too late and fallen asleep in the middle of an episode, and she couldn't wait to discover what happened next. Twenty minutes later, she had three strong theories and a guy beside her with tears in his eyes.

"Eight years and three kids. I came home from work, and they were gone." He wadded his cocktail napkin and kneaded it between his thumb and fingers. "Do you know how much lawyers cost?"

"A lot?"

"Yes, the bastards."

Chloe felt sorry for him. She hesitated then gave him a pat on the shoulder.

He took that as an invitation to hug. "Oh, I'm not much of a hugger." She pressed her palm to his chest and, with a firm push, wriggled free.

While her companion took a swig of his drink, Chloe shot an insistent look over at Luke. It was meant to convey something along the lines of *rescue me now, or I swear I'll lunge over the bar at your throat.*

He seemed to pick up on how things were going because he looked close to laughter as he looked down at his phone. Chloe's cell rang. "Hello?"

"Say 'Oh no!' Look shocked."

"Oh no!" She put on her best shocked face.

"Hang up and then say, 'It's the hospital. I've got to go.'"

Trying to appear truly distressed, she said, "Barry—"

"Barney."

"It's the hospital. I've got to go." She didn't wait for a reply. Luke was gone. At that point, she didn't even care where he was. She just wanted out. As the door closed behind her, she didn't have to look for him. She just followed the laughter.

"Come on, before he decides to follow you to the hospital to console you." He took her elbow, and they ran to the car.

Chloe collapsed in the seat. "You've got a cruel streak. What took you so long?"

"I was in my own private purgatory."

Chloe grinned. "Yeah, I saw." She half sang her next words. "You and your lady friend."

He looked sideways at her while he started the car.

As he pulled out of the parking lot and headed in the opposite direction of home, Chloe said, "I'm willing to concede that you're right. I was able to meet a guy at a bar. So now we can go home."

"Not a chance."

CHAPTER SIX

THE NEXT PLACE WAS A SKIERS' hangout at the foot of a nearby ski resort. The first place hadn't worked out as planned, but a place full of skiers would have to have one or two interesting prospects for Chloe... he hoped.

Before they got out of the car, Chloe turned to Luke. "Change of procedure."

He lifted an eyebrow. She had to be kidding. No, he could see that she wasn't.

Chloe looked him in the eye. "You took way too long at the last place. This time, I want you within earshot so you can hear and feel my pain. And I want a safe word."

A safe word. He tried not to shake from the laughter he was silently suppressing. "Okay. What?"

She pondered for a moment. "I don't know. Uh... well, we'll be in a bar, so... mahogany."

Luke was still far too amused. "Mahogany. Got it."

Inside, the bar was not nearly as crowded as the first

one, and it was nicer. He'd planned it that way. Chloe would up her game, building her confidence as they upscaled their surroundings. So by the time they reached the last bar, he could prove his point—that she would have much better results meeting men in real life than on a phone app.

So what if it hadn't gone well up until then. By the end of the evening, she would probably forget the first place, and his point would be made. The more thought he gave his scheme, the better he liked it. He hadn't taken it too seriously at first, but the plan had some merit. He liked Chloe. He had liked Eleanor, too, but he didn't want to see Chloe wind up like her aunt, with so much to offer and no one to receive it. Eleanor had always said she enjoyed her own company, but that was what he said when people queried him about his own choices. Of course, he had his own reasons for being alone. Eleanor had had hers, too, but she'd also confessed that sometimes she was lonely. That was one of the things they'd both had in common. They had understood each other and provided a friendship that was dependable without being a burden. Eleanor had managed just fine on her own, but Luke still thought she would have been better off with some family in her life. They wouldn't have needed to be close, but family would have given her some emotional support.

Chloe was young. She didn't have to live her life alone. But as he considered her life, he realized how foolish he was being. She had to have plans for her life. She didn't need him as her life coach. So why was he so determined to help her, assuming that was what he was doing? *If not, then what am I doing?* Chloe didn't need him. She was clever and creative, with too much to offer for someone not to notice and appreciate her. After all, he had noticed. Maybe if things were different, he might have taken an interest in her. But he was all wrong for Chloe even if she was all right for him. Still, the least he could do was honor his friendship with Eleanor by helping her niece. She had been a good friend, and he was just paying it forward.

Yeah, you're a friggin' saint, Abbot.

They found seats at the bar and settled into a nearly perfect seating arrangement, with Luke at the end of the bar and Chloe around the corner to his left. She had already ordered a drink by the time he arrived and slid onto his stool. He exchanged some small talk with the bartender then assumed the well-practiced look of a random loner at a bar.

The bartender was a young guy who appeared barely old enough to be serving liquor, but he seemed smooth enough as he chatted with Chloe. She laughed at something he said, then he left to take care of someone at the opposite end of the bar. With perfect timing, a guy slipped into the empty seat between Chloe and Luke. Not only did he position himself so that his back was to Luke, but Luke had to move to avoid the guy's elbow as he took his seat at the bar. Luke leaned over to get a better look at the guy's face, but the man's square jaw was in the way.

Luke knew his type. He'd gone to school with

dozens like him—a prep school, participation-award type whose helicopter parents bought their son's way into an Ivy League school. The guy undoubtedly played racquetball on weekends and had a place on Martha's Vineyard—waterfront, silver-shingled, and walls papered with money. Luke had worked his ass off and borrowed his way through school, while this guy had probably sailed through playing beer pong and turning in papers from the frat house files.

The guy threw his head back and laughed, giving Luke a better view of his face. Just as he'd thought—confidence like that was no accident. The dude was good-looking, with an easy smile that concealed what a bastard he was.

"Are you new in town?" Since the guy still had his back to Luke, he didn't see Luke roll his eyes. Chloe did, but she looked away quickly.

She said yes, sounding disgustingly chirpy. Luke was surprised she could see past the blinding sheen of the guy's perfect blond hair and the glint of white teeth. *Easy there, Chloe. If you keep smiling like that, you'll have to ice down your cheeks.*

"I'm Easton Amberson."

Of course you are. Luke leaned back and tried not to look like he'd swallowed sour milk.

"But my friends call me E."

Luke smirked. *Aw... that's as far as they've gotten in the alphabet, is it?*

Easton and Chloe chatted about where she was from and what she did. He'd grown up in the area and gone to Yale University. He now worked for an invest-ment firm. *Shocker.* He continued with the usual banter, dropping money code words. *Oh, got it wrong—there's no summer home on the Vineyard—it's on Nantucket.* The guy was so predictable, Luke could practically mouth the words along with him.

When Luke could stand it no more, he leaned over and interrupted. "Excuse me, but I've got this bet with a buddy of mine."

Chloe's eyebrows drew together while Easton turned toward Luke.

"What would you say this bar is made of?"

Easton gave him a skeptical look. "Oak?"

Luke nodded thoughtfully then looked at Chloe. "What do you think?"

She stared almost blankly but with pointed annoy-ance. "I don't know. Walnut?"

Luke tilted his head. "Really? I would have thought maybe... mahogany."

Chloe wrinkled her nose. "No. I don't think so."

Luke narrowed his eyes. "I think it is."

Easton leaned toward Luke and scowled. "Look, why don't you go home and query your browser?"

Luke glared back. "I think I will." He got up and left, shooting Chloe a look as he passed. On his way out, he pulled out his phone and paused at the door long enough to hear Chloe's phone ring. Then he went out to the car.

A minute later, Chloe stormed out and got into the car. "What was that about?" She slammed the door.

Luke gripped the wheel and stared straight ahead. "I didn't like him."

She lifted her chin. "Oh really? I did. And I'm the one who's going to go out with him."

With a sharp turn of his head, he asked, "What?"

She smiled and waved a business card in the air.

"Let me see that."

She handed it to him. "Go ahead. Keep it. We've already put each other's numbers in our phones. And they're synced to the cloud, so don't bother trying to get at my phone to delete it."

"He's not good enough for you." *Abbot, you're being an ass.*

Chloe's tone softened. "What's wrong? Wasn't that the whole idea? To get me a date?"

"No! It was to prove that you're better off meeting someone in person than through some stupid app on your damn phone."

"Someone sounds cranky," she said pleasantly.

"I just think it was a bad idea. Let's go home."

"Why? I'm having fun."

I'm not. But why was that? *I'm overreacting. So she met someone. Wasn't that the whole point of the outing? Get a grip.* "Sorry. I just didn't like that guy Weston."

"Easton. And yeah, I picked up on a subtle steely insolence with a hint of earthy abhorrence."

"You should write wine descriptions."

Chloe's eyes twinkled. "Thank you."

He couldn't stand her liking Weston, and he hated how that repugnant son of a plutocrat had latched on to her like a leech. But Chloe didn't seem to mind it, so making an issue of it would only make things worse.

Luke forced a chuckle and tried to diffuse the tension he had created. "He probably reminded me of some guy I once knew."

Chloe shook her head. "Poor guy."

"I'm okay."

A smile bloomed on her face. "I meant him."

Luke smiled back. "Yeah, well..." He looked outside —anywhere but at her. There was nothing to do but follow through with what he'd started. "Let's forget about Weston."

"Easton."

"Whatever. Bachelor Number Two. Anyway, I've got one more place to go. You're going to love this."

Her hopeful expression was unconvincing. "Okay."

As he approached the five-star hotel, a gut-churning feeling overwhelmed him. Maybe he'd pushed things too far, or maybe he was just getting tired of their game. His fun way to prove a point hadn't worked out as he'd expected. He'd meant to help Chloe broaden her horizons beyond her phone app and prove there was more to life than dating profiles and algorithms. She was an artist—she should understand that. There were subtle and extraordinary aspects of life that could not be reduced to a series of binary zeros and ones. She deserved more in life... in a relationship. And she was Eleanor's niece, which was the only reason he even cared. It made her almost like a cousin in his eyes. *Then why am I feeling so... not like a cousin?* When, during the evening, had he had a change of heart—or mind, rather? There was no heart involved—just the mind. And he minded the whole turn of events. He was bored with the game, and he wanted to go home.

Chloe gasped as they pulled into the parking lot of a grand Victorian hotel that had had a recent high-end renovation. "It's gorgeous!"

Luke smiled. "I thought you might like it." He'd been there during the holidays before, and with Chloe's love of everything Christmas, he'd thought its Victorian charm might appeal to her.

She wasted no time getting out of the car. He waited until she was halfway to the entrance, then he exhaled and followed. He had to admire her resolve to see their challenge through to the finish. In that respect, he had lost. He didn't even care about winning the game anymore, which was so unlike him. She, on the other hand, looked like her typical joyful self as she walked through the door with her usual cheer.

It's too late now. Here we go. Round three.

CHAPTER SEVEN

IF AUNT ELEANOR hadn't appeared to trust Luke, Chloe might have been more reluctant to do so. But they had exchanged keys, his number was the first on her aunt's list of emergency numbers, and Chloe had found a few random notes scribbled here and there to remember to give this to Luke or remind Luke about that. They had clearly been good friends, so if Eleanor had trusted him, she should too.

And why not? He'd been perfectly nice. But that night, he seemed different—still nice, but... different. She resisted the thought, but as the evening wore on, his attitude and behavior toward the men she encountered was beginning to look downright jealous. *Chloe, get over yourself. Why would he be jealous? He views you as a sister.* Supposing, however unlikely, that he did have feelings for her, why would he have spent a whole evening trying to get her a date? It wasn't the most brilliant strategy for winning a girl's heart.

If she was being honest, she'd had a sinking feeling when he had suggested the evening. Until then, she could not deny she had found him a little attractive. A lot, actually. Not that she was eager to do anything about it, but she found him extremely intriguing. She would have enjoyed getting to know him over time and possibly, eventually, discovering there was something between them, like an irresistible attraction simmering just under the surface. But that wasn't going to happen because he just didn't view her that way. Which was fine. He clearly wanted to be no more than friends. She was okay with that. She thought about it for a moment. *It's fine!*

She tried to preserve any air of sophistication she had by holding back a gasp as she walked inside the hotel. Dark marble and wood trim were all draped in fresh greenery, and a large tree stretched up to the two-story ceiling. The ambience was festive and elegant—everything Chloe loved about Christmas. A fire blazed in a massive white marble fireplace while soft lighting from wall sconces cast a romantic glow on the room and everyone in it. She glanced over at Luke. He looked even happier than she was.

She surreptitiously muttered, "Don't tell me you've caught some Christmas spirit."

"I'm just enjoying your reaction," he mumbled under his breath, gazing at her until she had to look away.

For some reason, she felt a little breathless. It must

have been the contrast in temperatures—coming in from the cold.

"See you inside." He walked away, admiring the Christmas tree.

Feeling somehow abandoned, Chloe walked into the bar. It resembled a cross between an old English pub and a Victorian library, with dark, polished wood paneling and finishes, a crackling fireplace, and decorative overhead beams. Luke had definitely saved the best for last.

Luke wandered in a few minutes later and sat three seats down from Chloe. She couldn't stop smiling. She loved it. She caught a whiff of pine garland and almost wished she could just sit there with Luke and talk. But as that thought occurred to her, a woman sat down between them. Oh well, he couldn't help it if he was a chick magnet. *Poor guy. Must be tough.*

"Is this seat taken?" a male voice asked.

Chloe turned to her opposite side to find a pleasant-looking man with a very nice suit and a warm smile to go with it. He looked very businesslike, pulled together all the way up to his neatly trimmed hair.

"No, help yourself."

With a charming nod, he did just that. He ordered a Scotch then turned to her. "Do you know this town well?"

"Well enough."

"What's your favorite thing to do here?"

"Honestly? Most of the things I love to do are at

home." *Oh, that was brilliant, Chloe! You sound fascinating already. Why not just tell him you're a homebody with twelve pairs of matching sweatpants, who enjoys coupon clipping and long walks to the pantry to feed her ten cats?*

Unfazed, he asked, "Such as?"

"I'm a painter—not of houses."

He looked duly amused. "Water? Oil?" He seemed genuinely interested.

"Watercolor, mostly." She met his soft gaze. *Hmm... those are very blue eyes.* If he were a superhero, those eyes would be his superpower, giving him the ability to take over the planet, or at least anyone on the planet who liked men. Luke had been right. Organic, in-person encounters were better. If she were on a dating app, she doubted this guy would have picked her. And she would have ruled him out as being not her type, maybe even out of her league. Yet there they were, talking. He was being charming, and she was charmed.

He leaned slightly closer. "I'd love to see your work."

Is that a pickup line? Does he want to see my etchings? She dismissed the thought. "I'm in the process of setting up a website." At least she was in the thinking-about-it part of the process.

"And what else do you like doing at home?" Unlike Chloe, he seemed calm and relaxed. And why not? Guys like that didn't have to work hard for attention.

Chloe grinned. "Well, at this time of year, I love decorating for the holidays." *Am I smiling too much? Looking too eager?*

He nodded with approval. "So you must love this place."

And maybe you if you keep looking at me like that. "I do." *Which is what I would say at our wedding.*

He looked up at the overhead beams decked with holiday garlands. "Is that mistletoe?"

She scanned the overhead decorations. There was plenty of fresh greenery gathered into gorgeous taffeta bows. "I don't see any."

He smiled bashfully. "Wishful thinking, I guess."

His head flew back as a fist struck his face, then he fell from the stool.

"Luke!"

Without answering, Luke wrestled with the man for a few tense moments then flipped the guy over and pinned him facedown to the floor. He barked out to Chloe, who without thinking, still gripped a glass in her hand. "Chloe, don't drink that!" Then he turned to the bartender. "Save that drink as evidence. Call the police and get me something to tie him up with." When the bartender hesitated, Luke said, "He just dropped something into this woman's drink."

The bartender emerged from her shocked state. "Okay, just a minute." She rummaged around under the counter, pulled out a roll of duct tape, and tossed it to Luke.

Once he had the guy's wrists and ankles secured, Luke got up and snapped instructions to the bartender. "Tell the police to send that drink to the lab. Here's my card if they have any questions."

Chloe was stunned, not only by the fact that a man had tried to drug her but by the sight of Luke's reaction. The other guy—he had never even told her his name—hadn't stood a chance. She'd never seen anyone act so swiftly or powerfully.

Luke put his arm around Chloe's shoulders and ushered her toward the door. "Come on. Let's go." He kept his face down as they passed a few onlookers with phones in their hands.

"Shouldn't we stay to give a statement to the police?"

"Later."

Chloe followed, still too stunned to do anything else. She spent the walk back to the car trying to figure out what had just happened. Luke barely spoke the whole way home, but Chloe picked up the slack, mostly from nerves. "I'm sorry. I never leave a drink unattended. I learned in college to always keep my hand over my drink when things feel... sketchy. But it was such a nice place. And he seemed so—"

"Nice?"

"Yes," she sheepishly answered.

Luke parked the car in her driveway. "It wasn't your fault."

Chloe thought about what might have happened and shuddered. "I would never have been here in this situation..." *If you hadn't dared me.* Fear roiled up inside her. "I don't do that. I don't go to bars, looking for men." She turned to him. "This was your idea." *Your fault.*

Luke said nothing.

"I don't know why I even let you talk me into this. Good night." Chloe got out and headed for the door.

He got out and started to follow, but she said, "I'm fine," and kept walking. When she got inside and closed the door, she leaned on it and exhaled.

LUKE WAITED until she was safely inside then went home. She was right. It was his fault. No argument there. And the topper was the scene he'd made in the bar. *So much for keeping a low profile.* With any luck, he had kept his head down or faced away from people's phones. But that would take luck. There was always a phone held by someone desperate to attain their fifteen minutes of social media fame in exchange for another person's dignity and ultimately their own.

Once inside, he started a fire, poured himself a glass of peaty Scotch, and put on his third vinyl record—he'd worn out two others—of the Argerich and Abbado recording of Ravel's Piano Concerto in G. He dropped the needle on the second movement, sank into his leather sofa, and stared at the flames as the right-hand melody hovered over a slow left-hand waltz, each hand slightly off from the other yet aching to find resolution.

AFTER THE PREVIOUS evening's debacle, Luke was determined to give Chloe some space. He took his morning run on the treadmill, which allowed him to look out through his rear window at the woods behind his house. The classic rock playlist he listened to when running did nothing to distract his thoughts from the previous night. He rolled his eyes to recall it.

Chloe blamed him. It wasn't that he didn't deserve it. He'd put her in that situation. But he hadn't planned how it had ended. It was just something that had happened. Random things happened. He'd protected her, though. And on the bright side, he'd rescued the next woman and the ones who came after, from that abusive pervert who would have preyed on them. But there would be a price.

The phone rang. He shut off the treadmill and looked at his cell. *That was quick.* "Abbot."

"We've got a project we'd like you to look at."

"Okay, I'll take a look."

"Not online. We need you here."

"For how long?"

"A few days, maybe a week."

Luke stared out at the trees. *Well, why not?* "Okay."

An hour later, he tossed a bag into his trunk and headed for the airport.

CHAPTER EIGHT

CHLOE GLANCED through the window at Luke's house while washing the dishes. She'd memorized his text message, not that it was hard to remember. *"Sorry about last night. I'll be gone for a week on business."* He was a regular Percy Bysshe Shelley.

But a week had gone by, so where was he? And why did she care? She didn't, not anymore. She'd been angry at first, justifiably so, then annoyed. But she had quickly remembered how swiftly he'd leapt to her defense. Wrestling wasn't her thing, but the sheer power with which he had wrestled that man to the floor—and at such close proximity—was impressive.

The whole takedown was a blur, finished in a matter of seconds. It had been so sudden and shocking that it wasn't until later, when she'd had time to reflect, that she realized how truly spectacular Luke had been. There was something primal about having him come to her aid in that way. Sadly, she would never be able to return the favor. Her self-defense skills extended as far as pressing the spray nozzle on a mace can. She really needed to do something about that. Meanwhile, poor Luke had been on his own.

As angry with him as she'd been when it happened, after a few days had passed, she arrived at a "no harm, no foul" view of the evening. It wasn't as though she'd been harmed. The worst she had suffered was a wasted twenty minutes of her time in a beautiful five-star hotel bar. The bet, or dare, or whatever it was, might not have been the most brilliant decision on either side, but it was over. It still bothered her when she thought of what could have happened if Luke hadn't been there, but then she wouldn't have been there at all if it weren't for him. The whole thing still felt a bit weird. *Lesson learned. No more social experiments.*

The incident did have an upside. Luke had stopped a predator from continuing to hurt other women. It was troubling to consider how many women would have been assaulted by that monster if Luke hadn't been so alert and sprung into action. When she'd given her statement to the police, they told her that her drink had, in fact, been drugged. They'd also mentioned that Luke had stopped by the station and given a statement. She wondered when that had happened. He must have stopped on his way out of town. The important thing was that a predator would have to account for his crime. She had to admit the situation had ended well.

She realized that Luke would never have let anything happen to her. For that reason alone, there were worse sorts to have as a neighbor. Aunt Eleanor must have figured that out about him, hence her obvious trust. That reminded Chloe of the key. She really needed to do something about swapping the house keys when he got back. Not that she didn't trust Luke. If a rabid bear or ruthless criminals broke into her home, Luke would be her first phone call from her hiding place under the bed. But she didn't trust anyone with her house keys, except maybe her mother, so she wanted them back.

She found herself counting the days he'd been gone, so his going away was for the best. It gave her time to calm down and acquire a philosophical attitude toward him. She was curious, though. He didn't owe her an explanation, but she wondered where he was. And that was the crux of the problem. She wondered too much about things, about Luke in particular. As Winston Churchill would say, Luke was a riddle wrapped in a mystery inside an enigmatic and staggeringly good-looking neighbor. Churchill might not have put it exactly that way, but the essence was there.

With one more look at the house across the road, Chloe exhaled and went to get ready. She glanced at her watch. She had an hour, which was time to shower, dress, and put on some makeup. She was going out on a date.

Slightly past noon, a car pulled into the driveway. Chloe waited at the door for the doorbell to ring, then she took a few slow breaths and opened the door. "Easton. Hi!" She grabbed her purse.

"Ready?" he asked.

As they walked to the car, he stopped and looked into her eyes. "You look nice."

Chloe felt heat rise to her cheeks. "Thank you." They gazed at each other for a moment as if frozen in time. Then a car engine broke the spell.

Luke pulled into his driveway. Chloe watched, but he didn't get out of his car.

"Shall we?" Easton touched her back lightly and gestured toward the passenger's side with his other hand. She got in, and they were off for an afternoon at a Christmas festival. Easton got it—Christmas and everything that came with it, including decorations and carols. They were meant for each other.

Chloe stole a wistful glance at Luke's parked car before Easton drove out of sight.

Happy Christmas to all, and to all a good night.

CHAPTER NINE

THE CHRISTMAS CRAFT fair was everything Chloe loved about Christmas. Kiosks were filled with every Christmas craft and gift item imaginable. They were never more than ten yards away from a food tent with treats like hot chocolate, eggnog, Christmas cookies, and pastries. A corner of the grounds was devoted to children, with cookie decorating, gingerbread houses, games, and face paint.

Easton bought two hot chocolates, then they found a bench and sat down. Chloe studied him as he told her about himself. He had the sort of square-jawed, athletic good looks one would expect of someone manning a yacht, with the positive outlook of one whose life had been sheltered from any negative aspects.

They arrived at the Ferris wheel, which they'd agreed to save for last since they both had a passion for them. When it started, Easton put his arm around Chloe's shoulders. It was sweet and romantic, yet Chloe found herself trying to figure out why she felt nothing. From the start, she'd had great expectations for what she and Easton might be together. They had so much in common. But looking at him was like gazing into a new picture frame or an outdoor-clothing catalog full of nice-looking strangers she felt nothing for. They might exhibit all the right features, but she had no desire to make out with any of them, which she realized as she took one more look at Easton was a crying shame.

She surveyed the grounds as they rounded the top of the Ferris wheel. What a perfect afternoon it had been. They'd acted like two kids without parental supervision, going from one ride or booth to the next. He was fun and companionable. Was the lack of chemistry between them some cruel trick of nature?

It began snowing. Easton turned to her with wonder in his eyes. "Could it get any more perfect?"

Chloe smiled. *No, with one glaring exception.* The snow floated down then melted when it landed on the ground. By the time they got off the ride, snow was beginning to cover every surface with a light gauzy coating. Easton took Chloe's hand, and they walked to his car.

They were quiet on the ride home, but it was a comfortable quiet. She liked that about Easton. He didn't force conversation. By the time he pulled onto Chloe's road, the snow clung to the branches, and the trees looked like lace. Everything was so beautiful, a perfect romantic vision.

There couldn't have been more than an inch of

snow on the ground, yet Luke emerged from his garage and began scraping his shovel over the driveway in straight, tidy rows. *Seriously?* It was as if he thought his all-wheel-drive SUV couldn't make it through in an emergency—for instance, if he ran out of beer.

Without turning her head, Chloe looked sideways at Luke as Easton made the turn into her driveway. He told her to wait then walked around to open her door. He offered his hand, and they walked hand in hand to the door.

"Thank you. It was such a nice afternoon."

Easton looked happy to hear it. "I'm glad. I enjoyed spending it with you." He glanced away almost bashfully then gazed into her eyes. "May I kiss you?"

For one moment, she wondered if maybe there was some untapped chemistry hiding under the surface and waiting to burst into unbridled passion. She had to find out. "Yes."

His kiss was gentle and nice, just like him. He even knew just when to end it. She hoped she did, too, because they, as a couple, were not going to happen. What had she expected—that his kiss might awaken her hormones like some sort of modern-day Sleeping Beauty? It hadn't. She didn't feel a thing except that she liked him and truly regretted not feeling more.

"Easton?"

He gave her a boyish grin that probably made all the girls sigh.

"You're just amazing, but..."

He exhaled, looking relieved. "You too?"

Chloe held back. She didn't want to assume.

"It's okay. I think you're amazing too, but..." He laughed, and Chloe joined in.

Still laughing, she said, "I really did have a fun afternoon. You're fantastic, and I love anything Christmas."

"Me too." He gazed at her. "Maybe we could get together sometime, just as friends. I do like you."

Chloe nodded. "That sounds great."

With a resolved nod, he said, "Good." Then he held out his arms, and they hugged.

The loud scrape of a shovel cut into the silence. Chloe glanced over Easton's shoulder and caught a glimpse of Luke's glare a split second before he turned and went into his garage. The door hummed as it closed.

Chloe waved at Easton as he backed onto the road and drove off, then she went inside, poured a glass of wine, and sat at the kitchen counter. She wondered if it was by design that the stool where she sat was the ideal height to look out the window at Luke's house. She sipped some wine. His driveway looked nice. God knew that inch of snow would have really hampered his exit— the exit he wasn't going to need to make any time soon. She frowned. *And what is the deal with the shovel? Ernest Shackleton's ship didn't make that much noise when the polar ice crushed it. Probably.* She didn't actually know.

What she did know was that just when she'd decided to forgive Luke, he had managed to annoy her again. She rolled her eyes in frustration. The only thing for it was wine. She took a sip and, as she set down her glass, spied his house keys. *Well, those have to go, and I want my keys back.* She glanced at her wineglass. "Be right back." Pausing at the mirror, she grabbed her purse then dug out some lipstick. *Because my lips are dry!* Why would she care about how she looked?

One minute later, she stood outside Luke's door. She only rang the bell once before he answered. "Chloe, hi." He stepped aside so she could enter, then he closed the door.

Oh, don't look so surprised to see me. She was tempted to ask if she could borrow his shovel, but she refrained. "How was your week?"

"Good." His seemed distracted. "And yours?"

"Good."

"Have a nice day with Weston?"

She stared into his eyes, but she couldn't for the life of her tell if he was joking. *He had to be. Didn't he?* "Easton."

As he nodded, his mouth twitched at the corner. Okay, he *was* joking.

"Yeah, it was great," she continued. "We're getting married tomorrow." It just came out. She said it as if they were getting mani-pedis together. She held Luke's gaze with a straight face while his face went through some transitions.

He did a double take when he realized what she'd said. She could see the wheels turning before his eyebrows drew together. But his look of alarm was the best.

"Not really. We were going to go steady, but he couldn't find his class ring." She chuckled, but it didn't feel as good as she'd thought it would. That was probably because Luke wasn't laughing... at all. "I'm joking."

"Why would you do that?"

"I don't know." She lifted her shoulders. "To be funny?"

His only reply was a slightly confused but otherwise blank stare.

Wow, this is really... awkward.

"Have you been drinking?"

Her jaw dropped, then she closed it and peered at him. "Why would you say that?" She blew out a breath. "Two sips. Maybe three. Which reminds me, that's when I saw these." She fished the keys from her jacket pocket and held them out to him.

He stared at them but made no effort to take them. "Keep them. Eleanor and I exchanged keys in case of an emergency. I've got a set of yours."

"Yeah, so I figured. I'd like mine back if that's okay." *If that's okay? It had better be!*

He gave her a questioning look then went into the kitchen. A minute of small scraping and rattling noises followed that sounded like the shifting of contents in a very full junk drawer. He emerged with her keys, and they made the exchange.

"Look, Chloe, I can see you're still upset with me about that evening."

"No, not at all. I just wanted my keys back."

"I forgot they were there, to be honest. I'm sorry if it made you uncomfortable."

"No, it's okay. I just... well, anyway, we're good, right?"

"Sure." He didn't look good at all.

Chloe searched his eyes, wondering why the two of them couldn't seem to get anything right. *Because you made it awkward, Miss Give-Me-My-Keys-Back.* "Well, thanks. I should get back." She turned toward the door.

"Easton seems like a nice guy," Luke said.

"Yeah, he is."

He nodded, and she smiled half-heartedly. She walked back to her house, but she wanted to run. She would need another week on her own to get over the uncomfortable feeling in the pit of her stomach. Luke did that to her. No, the truth was she let him affect her that way, and she couldn't seem to help it. *Why is this walk home taking so long?*

When she arrived home and made it inside, she looked at her wineglass. "You and I have some thinking to do. Did I say thinking? I meant drinking."

CHAPTER TEN

CHLOE PAUSED to look past her easel and sighed. It was snowing, and she was painting. It didn't get any better than that. On her easel was a watercolor paper on which she'd sketched the view behind her house. She was ready to paint.

Her phone beeped with a weather alert. A snow-storm was coming. It had been on the news for a week, but the forecast had worsened. The foot of snow they'd been predicting had increased to two. She set down her brush and went to the window. The snow was at least a foot deep already. Chloe needed to shovel the driveway. It would take her forever to shovel a foot of snow. Even done in installments, two feet of snow would be over-whelming. She assessed the effort and time as if they were part of a math word problem, and the answer was no. She frowned as she faintly recalled seeing a busi-ness card in her aunt's kitchen drawer. She went to the kitchen and found it. Relieved, she dialed the phone.

Ten minutes later, she put down the phone. Her aunt's plow guy was booked. He referred her to two other buddies of his. They also had their hands full with their seasonal clients. She slumped down on the stool and stared at the counter. She should have planned ahead. After divulging in a full minute of regret, she got up and got dressed for some quality time in the snow. Aunt Eleanor kept a snow shovel in the garage, next to the door. Chloe grabbed it on her way out. *Duh. Gloves.* Shovel in hand, she went back for her gloves then stepped outside and stared at the task before her.

An hour later, she leaned on her shovel and surveyed her work. By her estimation, she'd finished about ten percent of her driveway. *Would it have killed them to build the house close to the road?* She picked up her shovel and resumed. Only nine or ten hours to go.

The rumble of a motor destroyed the one thing she'd been enjoying, the pristine stillness of fresh snowfall in a pine forest. She looked over at Luke, who was cutting a swath through his driveway with a big-ass snowblower. *I hate you.* She did her best to ignore him. *So what if I'm old school? I'll get the job done, and goddamn it, nothing under my upper arms will ever jiggle again.* But as she worked, she fantasized about the snowblower display she'd walked past without thinking on her way into the hardware store to buy light bulbs. *Any one of those bad boys could have been mine.*

Twenty minutes later, the rumble came closer. Luke waved for her to move out of the way. If the snowblower weren't so loud, she might have heard a chorus of angels. He proceeded to make quick work of her driveway. Mere minutes later, he waved and steered his snowblower back to his garage. Chloe was beginning to think that maybe it was time to put aside their past differences. The least she could do was send him a thank-you text.

She reached into her pocket for her phone, but it was not there. She realized she must have left it on the counter when she'd put on her gloves. Chloe went to the front door, which was locked. She could envision her keys as clearly as if she were inside. Her phone and her keys were on the counter inside, where it was warm. But she was outside in the cold and desolate wilderness.

This can't be happening. She tried the garage door, but it was locked too. Next, she trudged through the snow to the back door. She knew that one was locked. At that point, Chloe felt as if she were dreaming. She heaved such a deep sigh, she practically made snow— like she needed any more. There was something to be said for keeping a key under the doormat or exchanging keys with a neighbor. *Crap.*

Chloe walked back to the front of her house and looked in through the window. *Yup.* There they were, keys and phone. *Okay, think.*

Footsteps crunched through the snow. She winced. *No...*

"Everything okay?"

Chloe turned and faced Luke. "Yes. A-OK." *A-OK?*

"Okay. Well, don't let me keep you."

She tried to sound light and carefree. "You're not."

He hesitated, studying her. "Okay. Well, I guess I should be going." He turned away.

"Luke? Can I use your phone?"

He turned back with a look of surprise then patted his pockets. "It's in the house."

"Yeah, mine too." *Oops. I mean, err...* "It's dead." *Good save.*

"But your landline still works, right?"

Maybe not such a good save. "I don't need a landline. I've got my cell."

"You should keep it. The signal up here is spotty at best."

"Thanks. I'll do that."

He looked past her to the warm light that shone from the window. "It shouldn't take long to charge your phone just enough for a phone call. But if that doesn't work, you're welcome to come over and use mine."

"Okay. Thanks."

"No problem. See you later."

"Bye."

He didn't move. "You're locked out, aren't you?"

"Yes."

A light came to his eyes, but he didn't say a word. Chloe waited for him to point out that she wouldn't be in this predicament if she hadn't asked for her key back. To her surprise and tremendous relief, he didn't say it. God knew he could have. Instead, he stood for a moment, apparently thinking and probably savoring the moment. Then, with a crooked smile, he went to the door and looked at the lock. He tried to turn the handle. "Yeah, it's locked."

Chloe frowned. "I'm aware."

He took off his gloves and stuck them in his back pocket. Then he pulled out his wallet and took out two small metal tools no larger than unwound paper clips. He put one of them in the keyhole and tilted it slightly. Then he inserted the other tool with it. Using both tools, he pushed, pulled, and jiggled for several seconds. Then the handle turned, and he opened the door. "There you go."

Chloe stared. "How did you do that?"

He shook his head. "It's just something I've picked up along the way."

"Really? 'Cause that didn't come up in my college coursework."

He grinned. "Maybe you took the wrong courses."

"So getting my key back from you..."

"Cost us an extra half a minute."

"Great." The whole lock situation was unsettling, which must have shown on her face.

Luke's smile faded. "Look, if I wanted to break into your house, I'd have done so by now. But I didn't, and I wouldn't unless you needed me to. I promise."

It made sense, but it didn't make her feel any less vulnerable. "Anyone could do what you just did."

He nodded. "A lock is just your first line of defense."

What's my second? Chloe took in a breath, but before she could ask, he said, "Go on in and warm up.

And maybe hide an extra key somewhere in case I'm not around."

She put her hand on the doorknob and held the door open a crack, just enough to keep from locking herself out again. She turned to Luke, still fixated on how he had picked her front door lock.

"But don't hide it under the doormat or above the doorframe," he added.

"I guess I could hide it on top of the porch light."

He shook his head.

Chloe looked around, considering.

"Not in front," Luke said. "Someplace not near a door. Be creative."

Chloe was already imagining an evening in front of her computer, looking up the security products she was going to buy.

He regarded her amiably. "You still fretting about the door lock?"

"Yes."

"You'll be fine."

She doubted that.

"Look, go inside, make yourself a nice hot Irish coffee, and forget about it—until tomorrow when you can do something about it."

"Okay. It's forgotten." *I'm imagining my next home invasion.* "Bye."

Once inside, Chloe locked the door and went to her studio to paint. She looked around at the three glass walls. A thin layer of glass stood between her and whatever was out there. She set down her painting supplies and went to the kitchen, where she'd left her phone. She picked it up, stared at it, and looked up Luke's number. Good. It was there, just in case she needed it during the night. *You're being silly.* She put down her phone. *No, you're not.* She stared at the phone for several seconds. Quickly, she picked it up. "Call Luke."

"Hello?"

"It doesn't have to be human. A bear could come crashing through my solarium window!"

"Probably not gonna happen." She could have sworn she detected a smile in his voice.

"It's creepy."

"What's creepy?"

"Being here with my lame windows and locks. I mean, I may as well just leave everything open."

"You'd be cold." Yes, she could hear him smiling.

"I'm being stupid," Chloe said. "Never mind."

"I'm sorry I've scared you."

She exhaled. "Well, it's just that the whole lock demonstration was pretty impressive, by which I mean terrifying."

He didn't speak for a while, then he asked, "Wanna watch a movie?"

"I guess."

"Give me a minute. I'll be over."

"Okay."

She hung up. *What just happened?* She hadn't meant to invite him. She just thought she might feel better talking to someone. Now he was coming over. It was nice of him. She felt better already, but... yeah, he was just being nice.

SHE ANSWERED his knock at the door. "I made popcorn."

"Great! So what are we watching?"

She took his jacket and hung it on a hook by the door. "Anything that doesn't involve home invasion."

He laughed. They flipped a coin, and he got to choose first. For starters, they would watch an action movie. Chloe brought out a blanket to share as they sat on opposite ends of her sofa. They took breaks and argued about characters and plot, and they laughed. She couldn't even remember about what. She just knew it was funny and easy between them. Being with Luke was comfortable—except when she turned to reach into the popcorn bowl and glanced at him. She'd never noticed that tiny scar on his jaw. She leaned back on her side of the sofa and studied his face. What would happen if she traced that strong jawline to his lips and then kissed him? She would probably get the same treatment as that guy in the bar. She would be down for the count within seconds. He turned and noticed her staring at him, then he smiled until Chloe looked down. She turned her attention back to the movie.

A few minutes later, he leaned over for popcorn, and she caught a glimpse of another scar—not a hairline scar like the one on his jaw, but a thicker scar, about two inches long, above his ear and extending toward the top of his head.

He turned and saw her wide-eyed expression. "What?"

"Sorry." She averted her eyes. "It's just... that looks like it must have hurt."

He seemed almost annoyed. "Oh, that. I told you I'd had a TBI."

"Yeah, I just..." She didn't know how he could have fallen in that particular place, and she didn't know how to ask him. He'd been evasive the first time the topic had come up.

He picked up the remote and paused the movie. "A bullet grazed my head."

"That's a little bit more than a graze."

"Well, it's fine now. There's no lasting brain damage except the headaches and vertigo, but they say that should subside."

"They? Like guys at the bar?"

He laughed. "No, my doctors. Are we finished here? I'd like to see what happens next."

So would I, but I'm not talking about the movie. She was still stuck on the bullet wound.

The movie ended, and it was Chloe's turn to pick. She took pleasure in announcing the genre: rom-com. After some deliberation, they agreed on a movie and pressed Play.

❄

LATER, as poignant music played over the closing credits, Chloe slept. Luke got up and spread a throw blanket over her. For a few moments, he watched her sleeping peacefully before whispering, "Good night." As he left, he set the lock and pulled the door closed behind him.

CHAPTER ELEVEN

CHLOE AWOKE THE NEXT MORNING. A warm smile bloomed as she recalled her evening with Luke. Nothing had happened in any definable way, but it felt as though something had changed between them. If only for an evening, they had reached beyond their comfort zones and found they were better together.

She looked outside. Luke's car was gone. By the end of the day, when he hadn't returned, she realized he'd gone away. Where or for how long, she didn't know. But she missed him.

She knew from the faint ache in her heart that she was falling in love. There was no point in pretending it wasn't happening or in trying to hold it at bay. She entertained no delusions that anything real might come of it. But after being alone for so long, it felt good to have something to cling to—a feeling, a hope. Just the warmth that filled her when she thought of him made her feel alive in a way she hadn't been in so long.

But today he was gone. She could not pine all day, wondering where he was or what he might be thinking about her. She needed a distraction, something real in her life. The roads had been cleared, so she went to her studio and pulled out three of her paintings from the series of storage racks lining half the wall. She still felt amazed by how lucky she was to have a place like this to work.

After loading the paintings into her car, she headed for town. She checked the business card she had found in her aunt's things and went into the shop. It was packed with shelves of gift items and pottery from local artisans. She caught sight of the walls in the back, which were covered with paintings.

"May I help you?" Behind the counter stood a middle-aged woman with salt-and-pepper hair. Her wild curls were haphazardly scooped into a scrunchie and twisted into a bun.

"I hope so. Are you Laura?"

"I am."

Chloe set her portfolio and paintings on the floor, propping them up against the counter. "I found your card in my aunt's things."

The woman looked back at her with polite interest. "Your aunt?"

"Eleanor Dowd."

Laura's face lit with emotion. "Eleanor Dowd was your aunt?" Her eyes misted up. "I miss her so. And her work. Both were so lovely."

Chloe nodded, agreeing. She may not have known

her aunt, but the woman had left behind over four hundred paintings, all of which Chloe adored. "I was hoping you might look at some of my paintings. To sell on consignment."

"Of course! Let's take a look." Laura cleared off some papers to make room while Chloe lifted one of the paintings and set it down on the counter.

Laura put on her glasses and studied the painting with a critical eye, at times almost smiling, then drawing her eyebrows together. She glanced up at Chloe. "Where did you study?"

"Temple."

Laura nodded with approval. "Let's see the others."

Chloe lifted the next and went through the same silent scrutiny. After she had shown Laura the third, the shop owner said, "I'll take all three. You've got your aunt's talent. Of course, your styles are entirely different, but the talent is there. I'll take the second one for myself. What did you want for it?"

Laura didn't blink an eye at Chloe's asking price. She just pulled out her personal checkbook and wrote Chloe a check. "I'll hang these others, and as soon as I've got some space, I'd like to see what else you've got."

Chloe felt a bit stunned. "Sure."

Laura looked through Chloe's portfolio and asked about which ones were available for sale in the shop. She leaned closer and smiled. "Let's keep a running inventory of three, and we'll see how it goes."

Chloe nodded enthusiastically. "Okay."

"Do you have a card in case I need to contact you?"

Chloe wrinkled her face. "Not yet. I'm just getting settled, but I'm at my aunt's house. The number's the same."

"Got it. Oh, and I'll need a certificate of authenticity for each of these."

Chloe nodded. "Sorry, I've got those right here." She reached into her portfolio and pulled out a brown envelope. Then she pulled out the certificates and explained which title went with which painting.

When Chloe had finished, Laura reached out and shook Chloe's hand. "I am so glad to meet you."

"Me too." Smiling, Chloe left the shop. *My first sale.* She took in a deep breath and exhaled. *I'm a professional artist.*

CHLOE PULLED INTO HER DRIVEWAY. Luke's driveway was still empty. No one could say he was a homebody. Was disappearing without notice a habit of his? She rolled her eyes. *Notice? He's your neighbor. He doesn't have to check in with you.*

Spurred on by her first sale, she spent the afternoon painting and designing a business card. Then she researched how to sell her work online. She wasn't sure whether to simply sell prints or to venture into merchandising. Finally, she decided to begin with the prints and expand from there.

Painting was the only thing that could get her mind off her new feelings for Luke, and she immersed herself in it. For two days, she barely came up for air, and the painting went well. So did the business aspect of it. By the end of the third day, she had formed a clear idea of the direction her art business was going and the logistics of setting it up.

Outside, dusk was falling. Having arrived at a stopping point, Chloe suddenly realized she was hungry. She'd worked straight through the day, barely stopping, and she had forgotten to eat. She closed the door to her studio, feeling very accomplished, and went into the kitchen to scrounge up some dinner. As she searched the cabinets and fridge, the phone rang. Thinking it might be a sales call, she was tempted to ignore it, but she reached out, barely looking, and picked up the phone.

"Have you eaten?"

She knew the voice instantly and glanced out the window. Luke's light was on, and his car was in the driveway. Her heart soared. "No. I was just looking through my cabinets for something." She chuckled. "You're not stalking me, are you?"

"Sort of. I saw the light on in your studio, and I didn't want to disturb you."

"Oh. That was thoughtful of you."

"Let's go into town. I'm buying."

"Okay. Give me twenty minutes." Chloe hung up the phone. *Calm down. He's just hungry and doesn't want to eat alone.* That was exactly what she did not want to believe, but she was falling too hard, and she needed to protect herself.

She glanced at her phone for the time. How long had it been since she'd hung up? She had nineteen minutes, tops, to get ready. She kicked into gear, showered, and towel dried her hair. She realized as she pulled on her top and put in her earrings that she was happily humming Christmas carols. After a quick final look, she headed for the door but then stopped abruptly.

She didn't know if he was coming to her house or if she was going to his. If she waited for him to come over, it would seem like she was assuming it was a date. If Luke lingered at his house and she remained too long at hers, it would be awkward. *Chloe, don't overthink it!*

She pulled on her boots and coat, grabbed her purse, and checked for her keys. She would not forget those. She pulled open the door and came face-to-face with Luke, who was reaching for the doorbell.

They stared at each other for a second then laughed. Chloe said, "I wasn't sure if—"

"Me too. My fault." He smiled and gazed at her. "It's good to see you."

She didn't know what to say. Three days' worth of questions clouded her thinking, but she was still pleased to see him.

He tilted his head. "Let's go. I'll drive."

She hadn't heard him pull his car into her driveway, but there it was. She must have been drying her hair. He always seemed to catch her off guard.

After a short drive, they pulled up in front of a small bar and grill on the outskirts of town. The dining area was small, dimly lit, and romantic. But the glaring lights of an old fast-food joint would have looked just as romantic to Chloe in the mood she was in. She was happy to see Luke and to be with him.

After the server brought their drinks and took their order, Luke leaned forward. "So what have you been up to?"

She talked about her painting and the business she planned to set up. He was interested and asked all sorts of questions. When they'd thoroughly discussed it, she asked, "What about you? What have you been doing?"

He made a face. "Nothing as interesting as what you've just told me."

"Try me." She leaned forward, curious to hear.

"Work."

"What is it you do again?"

Before he could answer, their food arrived. Luke started to tell her how he loved the food there.

"Luke?" She realized she had sounded abrupt, so she softened her tone. "You didn't finish telling me what you've been doing." He hadn't started, but she wasn't about to split hairs.

"Didn't I? I was sure that I had."

"No. And I'm not really sure what you do for a living."

"I work for the State Department."

"Right. You're a data analyst."

He nodded.

"So data is pretty much online or on computers, isn't it?"

"Not necessarily." He regarded her for a moment as she stared at the scar on his head.

"I'm trying to figure out how dodging bullets fits in to your job duties."

"Oh, the gunshot."

"Yeah, the gunshot."

"Well, it usually doesn't. I'm fine now. It put me out of commission at work, at least temporarily. But I'm almost up to speed, so they've been calling me in to consult."

It made sense, she supposed—the work part anyway. She nodded. It still seemed so nebulous, but she didn't want to interrogate him on their first date... or dinner... or whatever this was. She still wasn't sure. But the gunshot wound was an issue she couldn't let go of. Aside from the question of why people were shooting at him, she didn't want to catch one of the strays. She took a few bites of her dinner then quietly asked, "How did you get shot?"

"Chloe, I'd rather not talk about it. Let's just say I got in the way of a bullet, but I'm okay."

"Are we okay? Is someone going to pull up in their car and open fire on us?"

"No! I would never put you in danger!"

Chloe thought about the scene at the bar.

From the look on his face, he was remembering it too. "Chloe, you're safe."

She was pushing too hard, and she didn't have the right. They weren't that close. As long as he was telling the truth, which she believed he was doing, he didn't owe her any more of an explanation than that.

She cleared her throat. "I don't mean to pry."

"It's okay. I didn't mean to make you feel uncomfortable."

But he did, however unwittingly. He had a mysterious bullet wound, and she didn't know why. And now she felt uncomfortable. Anyone would. For a while, they quietly focused on eating, occasionally managing to exchange a few shallow comments. They declined dessert, and Luke asked for the check. The car ride home wasn't much better.

Luke walked her to the door. "Would you mind if I kissed you?"

Mind? She had not expected that. "No."

He bent down and touched his lips softly to hers. When he pulled away, her head was spinning. *So that's what chemistry is.* She'd never known it would feel like a tsunami assaulting her senses. She gazed into his eyes, still reeling.

He smiled. "Got your key?"

"Yes!" One kiss and she'd lost her mind. "Yes, it's in here somewhere." She rummaged through her purse. Dammit, where was it? She checked her pockets and exhaled with relief as she held it up. "Got it." Judging from the glint in Luke's eyes, he was enjoying her key-searching frustration far more than she was.

She opened the door, and when she turned to say good night, he put his hand behind her head and kissed her again, longer and deeper than before. "Good night, Chloe."

She was surprised her voice came out at all, but she managed to squeak out "Good night" before he turned and left.

Chloe closed the door and put her hand to her chest. That guy was going to change her life. She just hoped it would be for the better.

CHAPTER TWELVE

Chloe sat at her desk and stared at the computer screen. The memory of Luke's kiss was destroying her morning's productivity. All thoughts led to Luke. Falling for her neighbor had not been the best choice. She went to the window and looked across the street. *Is he awake? Is he thinking of me?* That was crazy. At this rate, she would have nothing to show for the day but a striped sunburn from staring through the blinds, looking for him. "Striped Sunburn at Christmas." That might make a good country song.

Chloe needed some Christmas spirit and new scenery, so she got dressed and made plans to recoup her lost day. She drove into town, mapping out her afternoon as she went. She would start with some shopping. After that, she would treat herself to lunch then wander over, hot coffee in hand, to the Christmas tree in the town square. With any luck, she might catch a school choir singing carols. She felt better already.

She had made it through shopping and settled into a deli booth for some lunch when Laura appeared at her table. "Chloe! How are you?"

Startled from her musings, Chloe looked up and smiled. "Laura! Sit down."

"I just stopped by for a coffee, but sure."

As they chatted, Laura shared that some customers had already been admiring Chloe's paintings. An artist herself, Laura asked some questions about her influences and technique. Before long, Chloe was so lost in talk of art that she almost forgot about Luke.

Laura took care of that. "So, how are things with your new neighbor?"

"Luke?" That sounded convincingly casual... she hoped.

"Do you have another neighbor?"

Chloe laughed. "No, not really."

Laura wasn't shy or subtle. At the moment, that was a significant flaw. "So what's your take on him?"

Chloe tried to sound nonchalant. "I like him."

Laura nodded. "Of course you do. Every single straight woman in a ten-mile radius—and a few not so single... or straight for that matter—have given him some thought, if not their best effort."

Chloe wished she hadn't heard that. She had no appetite for competition, at least not for a man.

"I can't get a good read on him, though," Laura said.

Chloe shrugged. "He seems nice enough."

Laura grinned. "Nice enough? I may be out of the

game, but even I can tell he's more than just nice enough."

"I don't really know him that well." *Just well enough to let him kiss me again.*

Laura studied her for a moment. "You might want to check your pulse to make sure you still have one."

Chloe made a show of lifting her hand and touching her wrist. "Yup, still there."

Laura smiled and shrugged. "Just checking. I mean, it's none of my business, but he seems like a really nice guy. You two might be good together. Food for thought."

Chloe nodded half-heartedly.

"Well, I'd better get back to work. Merry Christmas!"

"Thanks." So, breaking news, Luke was attractive. What would she do without Laura?

THERE WERE no carolers at the tree in the square, but the tree was enough. It looked pretty against the backdrop of the Main Street shops all decked out for the holiday season. Chloe sat down on a bench and took in the sight of her new town. Aunt Eleanor knew how to pick them. Places like this ended up on Christmas cards. However, no town was quaint enough to make Chloe forget how cold a stone bench could feel in the winter, so she got up and headed back to her car's heated seat.

After she got home, she was pulling the last of her

Christmas shopping bags out of her trunk when a movement at the edge of the woods caught her eye. No, it wasn't a bear. It was... "Luke?" He emerged from the trees and tromped toward her. "Are those..."

"Snowshoes."

"I didn't know people still did that."

"Really?" He acted as though it were something she should see every day. "It's great exercise. They say it burns four hundred to a thousand calories per hour."

Chloe lifted her eyebrows. "My knee-jerk reaction is to say sign me up, but those burned calories must be hard-earned."

"They are. But it's fun. Want to try it sometime?"

Chloe tried to look optimistic. "I will definitely give it some thought." She smiled, certain he saw right through her.

He looked at the shopping bags in her hands. "Been Christmas shopping?"

She smiled and lifted the bags with a shrug.

His cheeks were still flushed from exertion, and his eyes were bright. Chloe's gaze fell to his lips, and once more, she recalled his kiss, which was on a video loop in her brain. She lifted her eyes to find his gaze fixed on hers.

"Are you busy tonight?" he asked.

Sadly, she was, and she told him as much. She thought hard about whether to suggest her next idea. "Are you familiar with *The Nutcracker*?"

His face went blank, which Chloe assumed meant he'd never heard of it. "It's a ballet. Tchaikovsky?"

He nodded. "Toy soldiers, rats, and sugar plum fairies?"

She laughed. "They're mice, but yes, that's the one. My mother runs a dance studio in Vienna, Virginia. Her students do the children's parts in a Washington production of *The Nutcracker*, so I'm going."

"My love of classical music hasn't extended to ballet. Yet."

She gave him bonus points for the effort. She hadn't really expected him to have any interest in ballet, but now she was encouraged. "I could get you in. I know people." The chances of him, or any guy for that matter, wanting to endure a ballet, let alone the long drive to and from, was unlikely, so she waited for the inevitable rejection.

"Okay."

"What?"

"I'm in."

"I heard you. I just can't believe you."

"Why not? You'll be there, won't you?" He looked into her eyes as if he were unwaveringly sure of his feelings.

She felt dizzy from the unexpected interest. "Yes."

In contrast, he looked so steady and sure. "Then yes, let's do this."

At the moment, she was practically melting. If he didn't stop looking at her like that, she might bypass melting and go straight to the next phase, in which she would jump him and have her way with him right there in the snow. She imagined the resulting snow angels.

Was it too early in their relationship for that? *Probably. Yes.*

"Okay." She looked at her watch. "Can you be ready in an hour?"

"Yeah. Wait. Do I need a tux?"

"No, a sports coat will be fine."

"Pants optional?" He gave her a devilish grin that made her heart skip a beat and her imagination go wild.

"No. I'm afraid there's a dress code." *Too bad about that.* Her face flushed as she averted her eyes for an instant. She looked back to find a mischievous look in his eyes. *Focus, Chloe.* She tossed off a quick, "I'll pick you up in an hour," then turned and escaped to her door. Behind her, the crunch of retreating snowshoes grew faint in the otherwise quiet afternoon.

What had she been thinking? Ballet? Was he really ready for that? Chloe hoped she hadn't just killed the relationship before it had started.

CHAPTER THIRTEEN

CHLOE LEFT Luke settled in his seat and went backstage to touch base with her mother. Judith Burke was in an intense tête-à-tête with the stage manager while frenetic young ballerinas stretched and flitted about. She gave her mom a quick hug, said the traditional *merde*, then left her to deal with what looked like a calamitous issue but probably wasn't.

When Chloe slipped into her seat, Luke asked, "Is everything okay?"

"It's exactly how it always is. My mom's really amazing in the way she corrals dozens of dancers ranging from toddlers to teens, but there's always some tension in the air before curtain." She looked into his eyes. "You have no idea what you've gotten yourself into, but I'm glad you're here."

"I am too."

"Yeah, well, remember you said that an hour from now."

He looked a little offended. "I think you're forgetting I like classical music. If I can listen to Prokofiev, I think I can take anything Tchaikovsky can throw at me."

"I stand corrected."

The curtain rose, and Chloe lost herself in the dance world she'd left behind years before.

During intermission, they walked out to the lobby and settled in an unoccupied corner. Luke leaned against the wall. "So your mother taught dance. Were you one of her students?"

"I was, from as young as I can remember until I graduated from high school." She glanced toward the theater. "I worked my way through nearly every part in the ballet, except Clara. Maybe that's what made me such a Christmas fanatic. I must have been about ten when I got my own personal video copy of *The Nutcracker*. I was well over bedtime stories by that point. Instead, Baryshnikov and Kirkland danced the pas de deux every night before bed. I was in ten-year-old love!"

"But you never played Clara?" He listened so intently, Chloe felt self-conscious.

She shook her head. "Aside from not being quite up to the task, I never liked being onstage. I loved the dancing but not the audience or the pressure. It just wasn't for me."

"But painting was."

She turned to him with a reticent smile. "Yes. I could do it alone and not have to think of anyone's reaction." She averted her eyes, ready to change the subject to anything but herself, then she turned back to him. "I still don't quite understand what you do."

"I try to spare people the boring details. By the time I do that, there's nothing left to tell."

She studied him with narrow eyes. "You're very good."

"At?" Chimes sounded to end intermission, and Luke offered her his arm. "Shall we?"

They returned to their seats, but Chloe couldn't get Luke's evasiveness off her mind. *What is he hiding?* It took the pas de deux to finally distract her. She'd seen *The Nutcracker* countless times, yet that part always brought tears to her eyes. This time, it gripped her. It was the embodiment of everything romantic, while at the same time, it was everything that real life could not be. Two people meant for each other drew together, their hearts and bodies soaring. The stage was clear. Nothing stood in their way. They were open, honest, and free with each other, leaping and soaring along with the music. And he always caught her. If she fell, it would only be into his arms.

A tear trailed down Chloe's cheek. Luke looked over. While others applauded, he gently brushed it away.

Afterward, there was a flurry of activity as they made their way backstage. Her mother was beaming. "We've pulled off another one." She made a face that made Chloe laugh.

"Mom, this is Luke."

Her mother raised an eyebrow.

"My neighbor," Chloe added in a tone that said *back off*.

"Luke, it's so nice to meet you."

Luke flashed a smile. "Thank you, but the pleasure is mine, Mrs. Burke. And what you've done with the ballet! Tchaikovsky would have been proud."

Chloe's mom laughed. Chloe knew her too well. That she liked Luke was now a given. She could see the wheels turning. Chloe hesitated then asked, "I don't suppose you could join us for a drink?"

Her mother shook her head. "Matinee tomorrow."

"I figured. Well, good luck with the rest of the run." They hugged.

Luke had charmed her mother, of course. Regardless of what happened between Luke and Chloe, she knew she would be hearing his name for weeks. But she couldn't really blame her.

Before facing the two-hour drive home, they stopped for a couple of large take-out coffees. While they waited in line, Chloe stared at the menu, trying to decide if she wanted something to eat.

"Dave? David Bertram."

She tuned out the man's voice, along with the other nearby conversations, until Luke answered. "Hi. How are you?"

She turned to find Luke engaged in conversation with a man who clearly thought Luke was some guy named David Bertram. *Mistakes happen, but why wouldn't Luke correct him?*

With a frown, Chloe turned and watched the two men chat. Luke didn't introduce Chloe. For all the other man knew, she was just a stranger standing in line behind him. They went through the usual small talk. The other guy had a bag in his hand and was on his way out.

"May I help you?" asked the server at the counter.

Chloe glanced distractedly back at Luke then ordered two coffees while the men said their goodbyes. She told him she'd ordered for him, and they silently waited for their coffees.

On the way back to the car, Luke looked at Chloe. "You okay?"

She wasn't.

"Want me to drive?" he asked. "It's my turn."

After a moment, Chloe said, "Okay," and went to the passenger's side.

Luke started the engine and fastened his seat belt.

"David Bertram? Or should I just call you Dave?"

He leaned back and chuckled. "I know. That was weird. We worked on a project a while ago. Dave Bertram was on our team too. He obviously mixed our names up. No harm, no foul."

"Yeah." She stared at the parking lot as Luke backed out of their space and pulled onto the road.

"So you were a ten-year-old ballerina," Luke said. "What else? Rugby? AV club?"

"Band. I played the bassoon."

"Really? I would not have guessed that."

"Oh?"

"I had you pegged for a flute player."

"The flutes were all taken. But I wound up liking the bassoon. I'm more comfortable hiding in the middle, heard but not seen."

He stole a sideways glance. "I'm noticing a theme here."

"But the double reeds are a bitch."

He laughed. "Really? I had no idea."

She nodded. "It's amazing how everything can be perfect, but a little reed can throw everything off."

He made a barely perceptible turn in her direction. "Yeah, I can see that. The devil's in the details."

Chloe stared straight ahead. "Like a name."

He didn't move, and he didn't say a word.

That was the moment that Chloe was sure—sure enough not to press it any further. Luke Abbot was not who he seemed to be. Every question she'd ever asked him raised more questions. Her imagination ran wild until she realized how vulnerable she was. She was alone in a car with a man who had secrets. It was her car, but she had relinquished control. When they got home, he would be there, right across the road from her. He'd already demonstrated how useless her locks were. *Locks.* She looked at the car door and rehearsed an escape if she found herself needing one.

She was being silly. Imagination was the blessing and curse of the creative. Luke had been perfectly lovely all evening. He'd been polite to her mother, and he had wiped her tear. How could that same man ever harm her? Yet how could the same man have secrets—secrets involving gunfire?

After an hour, she offered to drive, but he said he was fine. The rest of the car ride was quiet except for the radio music. Chloe should have felt some relief when they pulled into her driveway, but she didn't. An hour of near silence had heightened the unspoken tension between them.

Luke parked the car and handed Chloe the keys. She tried not to let her relief show as she took them. She toyed with the idea of waiting until he was home and then driving away. To where, she didn't know. It wasn't as though she had unlimited funds to move into a hotel until she figured out what Luke was hiding from her.

They got out of the car. "It's late," Chloe said. "I've kept you out long enough."

"Chloe, is something wrong?" He'd obviously picked up on her discomfort, but he did not seem surprised. She had the distinct sense he'd been through a similar situation before. "I would never hurt you." He couldn't have said anything worse.

"I know that." She didn't. He had just thrown fuel on the fire of her fears, all but confirming there was good reason behind them. Even if he wasn't involved in anything dangerous, he was hiding something from her, and it made her uneasy. But he would never hurt her. She was supposed to believe that because he had just said so. No, she did not find that calming. "Well, good night."

If she could have made a grand jeté to the door, she would have. She couldn't put distance between them fast enough. With a huge sigh, she made it inside and leaned against her door—the one with a lock he could pick in less than thirty seconds. Aunt Eleanor hadn't installed a security system, so Chloe added that to her to-do list. In the meantime, she went to the pantry, pulled out a couple of wine bottles from the recycling bin, and propped them on top of the front and back doorknobs. In theory, if someone broke in, the bottles would fall and make enough noise to alert her to an intruder.

She did not sleep well that night.

CHAPTER FOURTEEN

THE NEXT MORNING, Chloe went to the hardware store and bought a do-it-yourself alarm system and new locks for the doors. She'd just finished installing the alarm system when the doorbell rang. She looked at her phone app and saw Luke. The front door camera worked. How well would it work if she opened the door and Luke's secrets turned out be crime related? If she didn't open the door soon, he would think something was wrong. She was making it weirder. Her phone app had a panic button. She would keep it handy just in case.

She opened the door and tried to look pleasant, but it felt strained. Hopefully, he couldn't see it in her expression. "Hi."

He smiled. "I've got some Jamaican Blue Mountain coffee." He glanced toward his house. "Would you like to come over for a cup?"

After all of her efforts to turn her cabin into Fort

Knox, she wasn't about to risk going to his house voluntarily. "Luke."

His expression changed as if he knew what was coming.

"I need to take a step back," she said.

He raised his eyebrows. "Oh?"

She hadn't planned what she would say, but his silence made her uncomfortable, so she fumbled her way through an explanation. "It's me. I got ahead of myself. I'm trying to start a new life and a business. I'm a bit overwhelmed right now, so..."

"Was it that guy at the fast-food place? He just got my name wrong. It's a simple mistake."

"No. Maybe. I don't really know you, do I?"

With a half smile, he said, "I've been working on that."

She found herself smiling back, which undermined what she was trying to do. She forged onward. "You're a great guy."

He laughed, and it threw her. The next second, his laughter was gone, and a cynical look took its place. "So you're giving me the 'but' speech?"

"What?"

"You know. 'You're... fill in nice thing, other nice thing, but...' The breakup compliment sandwich."

She managed to face him. "I'm sorry."

"I am too." The look in his eyes broke her heart. He walked away, and that broke her heart too.

Chloe had a sudden urge to go after him. What had she done? She didn't know for a fact that he was involved in anything bad. She was guessing, protecting herself. But she didn't know anything about him at all. The mere fact that he was so secretive was a red flag. He had something to hide. It didn't matter, at that point, what it was. People didn't go out of their way to hide good things. And they didn't have random people coming up to them and calling them by some other name. Whatever Luke was—drug dealer, gangster, or hit man—it couldn't be good.

Yet even knowing he was hiding something, she still felt a connection between them. *What's the matter with me?* She still longed to be with him. If only they could shut out the world and be together. Seeing him that morning had made her feel almost certain—almost—that he would never hurt her. But no one could live a secret life forever without someone intruding and bursting the bubble. This time, it was some guy saying hello to someone he knew as Dave. But the next time might involve someone who posed a danger to Luke. Or to her. She would be crazy to get involved with someone like that. No, she'd done the right thing.

If only they weren't neighbors...

CHLOE STOPPED by Laura's gift shop to drop off some of her new business cards, and she left after promising to wrap gifts in the church basement later that afternoon. Who could say no to needy children at Christmas? So they met up after lunch and walked over together.

They were a formidable pair in the wrapping department. As Laura finished wrapping another gift, she leaned over to Chloe. "Now, doesn't this feel better than shopping?"

Chloe wouldn't have even tried to deny it. "It does." It was also a perfect distraction from Luke, except during moments when his name came up.

Laura studied Chloe for a moment then returned her gaze to her wrapping. She made a horrible attempt at sounding nonchalant. "Did I see you with Luke the other day?"

Chloe swallowed then continued wrapping as she tried to frame her words in a way that would politely discourage discussion.

"Luke?"

"You know. Luke, your neighbor."

Chloe felt her cheeks heat. "Yes, you did. But you won't anymore." *Wow, Chloe. Way to discourage discussion.*

"Oh?" Laura sounded disappointed.

"Yeah."

"Sorry." Laura continued her wrapping. "My matchmaking skills must be rusty. I thought you'd be so great together. "

Chloe kept her eyes on the ribbon she was tying. "So did I, for a while. But there are too many missing pieces." She lost her grip on the ribbon and started again.

Laura lifted an eyebrow. "Such as?"

Chloe shook her head, wondering where to begin. "He knows all about me, and yet I know nothing about him."

"So he's a good listener."

Chloe sighed. "It's not like I haven't asked questions. Anyway, I just needed to put on the brakes."

"Eleanor thought the world of him." She set down the package she was wrapping and looked straight at Chloe. "What really happened?"

Chloe couldn't blame Laura for being curious, but she wished her new friend would leave it alone. "Why does it matter? Did he put you up to this?"

Laura leaned away, stunned.

Chloe hadn't meant to snap. Almost as stunned as Laura, she said, "I'm sorry. I don't know where that came from. I guess you hit a raw nerve."

"Actually, I have spoken with Luke," Laura said softly.

Why? Chloe wanted to whine, but she'd done enough damage. She sat quietly, waiting for what would come next.

"I've known Luke for a long time. You can trust him." Laura said it with the intuitive sense Chloe had noticed before. Laura was an observer. She picked up on people's emotions and interests, which was why she was so good at matching people with paintings.

"Did I say that I don't?"

"Do you?"

"No." Chloe glanced around, in part wishing the

subject would change yet desperate to talk to someone. She considered her choice of words, unsure how much of what she said would get back to Luke. "He's got too many secrets. That's not a good sign. And that's just not what I'm looking for in a... relationship."

"I can see how he'd strike you that way," Laura said thoughtfully.

"It's not just that he's private or reclusive. There are things about him that just don't match up. And when I ask him, he's very skilled at avoiding an answer. To be honest, it's a little bit scary."

Laura didn't seem surprised. "Ask him."

"I've asked him so many things."

Laura's look of concern was reassuring. "I think a lot of the two of you, and I'd hate to see you miss out because of a misunderstanding."

That's not up to me, is it? She wanted to say it, but instead she accepted Laura's advice. The woman had been very kind to Chloe, and she clearly was trying to help.

The subject soon changed, to Chloe's relief, and the gifts were eventually wrapped. Children would have gifts from Santa, and that made Chloe happy. It was time to go home and face life. But the whole way there, Laura's words echoed in her ears. *"Ask him."*

As if she hadn't. But getting him to answer was another thing altogether.

CHLOE'S HOUSE lights came on, and Luke couldn't help himself. He went to the window and looked across the road. She went into her studio and sat at her water-color easel. He took a sip of his Scotch and turned from the window. He was better off back in his chair, staring at the fire.

He liked to think he had simplified his life by avoiding love over the years. He probably had, but that was just a positive spin on the truth. Any time he had dated, the relationships always ended sooner or later. His job complicated things, but he could have worked through that. The truth was, he had never been tempted to let himself love someone deeply enough to risk it. He'd never said those three words to anyone.

Chloe was different. He'd known from the moment he met her that she wasn't like the others. He'd known early on that whatever happened between them would leave an impression. He let out a cynical chuckle. He'd come to believe it would be love, but at the moment, all he had were bruises—to his ego as well as his heart. As if testing the relationship to see if it was real, he'd taken his time getting to know her. He'd been in no hurry. In fact, he wanted to savor the process of falling in love and discovering everything that he could about her. And for practical reasons, he wanted to be sure not only of his feelings but of hers. If they arrived at the critical point of commitment, he had to be sure it was right and that she would have no doubts.

Chloe was not on a parallel track. She had gone straight to questions and doubts. She seemed to have drawn some conclusions about him, which were wrong. If she knew him at all, she couldn't have suspected him of anything but caring for her. He'd always prided himself on being good at reading people, but he'd gotten it so wrong with her. She didn't look at him and see his character and integrity, and that hurt. He could learn to accept it, but he couldn't seem to stop falling in love.

CHAPTER FIFTEEN

CHLOE MADE A MISTAKE. With an exasperated curse, she crumpled up her watercolor painting and hurled it across the room. That wasn't like her, but neither was the uneasiness that she couldn't shake off. That was her last piece of watercolor paper, but Aunt Eleanor had stockpiled some supplies in the attic, so she headed up the stairs to retrieve them. Although Chloe had sorted and cleaned out the rest of the house, she hadn't spent very much time in the attic. There wasn't much there, only some stacked boxes, all the exact same size. The few she'd looked into contained old china and dishes, most likely family heirlooms. She made a mental note to see if her mother recognized or wanted any of them.

At the end of the attic was a wall of shelving, most of which contained paper and stretched canvases in a number of sizes. The attic was Aunt Eleanor's warehouse. In the center was a bookshelf. One shelf was dedicated to black sketchbooks containing Aunt

Eleanor's work. Going through those would make for a nice afternoon. The next shelf contained a book of essays by artists, several books about the creative process, half a shelf on art history, and a book on the business of building a painting career. On the end, clearly misshelved, was a leather-bound copy of Charles Dickens's *A Christmas Carol*.

Chloe reached out and tried to take it from the shelf. As she pulled, the book tilted outward and released a spring that propelled the shelf toward her. It was the door to a secret room. Chloe opened it the rest of the way then took her phone from her pocket and turned on the flashlight. "Aunt Eleanor, what are you hiding in here?"

She spied a light switch and turned it on. It illuminated a small room with a chair and a wall of built-in cabinets. Inside one of the cabinets was a gun safe and above it, a small backpack. Chloe unzipped the pack and began taking out items. First, she retrieved a small water bottle and snack bar. She wondered how old that was. Next came a hat, a small first aid kit, and a toothbrush. She'd obviously stumbled upon her aunt's hiking backpack and was about to set it aside when she felt something familiar in one of the pockets. No one went hiking with a passport, let alone three—US, Canadian, and UK—all bearing her aunt's photo. There were three envelopes containing US and Canadian dollars and British pound notes. Several folded maps were bundled together with an old, hardened rubber band that had partially melted onto one of the maps. At the bottom of the backpack was a change of clothes and a rain jacket folded into a pouch. She had stumbled upon some sort of getaway kit.

Forgetting about the watercolor paper she'd come for, Chloe shoved everything back into the pack, closed the secret door, and headed downstairs. She clutched the backpack to her chest and paced back and forth in her kitchen. What was this? Who was her Aunt Eleanor, really? Her aunt seemed as mysterious as Luke. She thought about what good friends Luke and Aunt Eleanor had been. She'd thought that was so nice. Luke had looked out for her aunt. But she wondered if there was more to it than that. It seemed oddly similar that the two "friends" harbored secrets. Could Luke know that his sweet, elderly neighbor had a secret room with a gun safe and an assortment of bogus passports? Something was not right, and Chloe was determined to find out what it was.

It just didn't make sense. Laura had known and liked Aunt Eleanor, but Laura may not have known of her aunt's secret side—the one with hidden guns and multiple passports in the attic. And then there was Luke. Aunt Eleanor had been a bright and intuitive woman, yet she hadn't seen Luke as a threat, nor had she been bothered by his secrets—if she knew them. *Ask him.* That was what Laura had told her.

Before she lost her nerve, Chloe slipped on the backpack, not even bothering to put on a jacket, and marched over to Luke's house. She rang the doorbell then knocked. When the door opened, she pulled off the backpack and held it out to him. "What is this?" she demanded.

He stepped aside and invited her in. "What are you doing? It's freezing out there."

She shook her head, too preoccupied to care. "It's a short walk."

He took the backpack and led her to the sofa that faced the fireplace, then he put a throw blanket over her shoulders. "Now, what's this about?" He sat down beside her.

"Go ahead. Open it. Take everything out and then tell me what that is."

He pulled out the passports and looked at each one, then he glanced at the money and spread the rest of the items out on the coffee table. "Where did you find this?"

"Aunt Eleanor had a secret room in the attic. This backpack was in it. I don't even know what to make of it."

"It's a go bag." He answered her questioning look. "It's a bag of essentials in case she had to go somewhere quickly."

"And why would my elderly aunt need a go bag?"

"Your aunt wasn't the frail, shawl-covered elder you're imagining. But for what it's worth, the passports expired a decade ago. It's probably been even longer since she used that bag."

Chloe just stared at him. She was done with the secrets. He knew something, and she was going to find out what it was.

Luke appeared gravely concerned.

"I need to know," Chloe said.

"Chloe..."

"Everything you've been keeping from me. It's not just about you—it's about my aunt. Am I even safe in my house?"

He leaned forward and sighed. "This can't go outside of these walls."

Chloe shivered and clutched the blanket tighter around her shoulders.

"Your aunt had a particular—"

Chloe rolled her eyes. "Don't tell me. My aunt had a particular set of skills? Really?"

He looked perplexed.

"I mean it, Luke. Tell me the truth."

"She knew art, with a... specific area of expertise that was valuable."

"To whom? What was she, an art forger? A thief?"

Luke leveled a look that bore through her. "She worked for the CIA."

Chloe burst out laughing. "Oh, c'mon. You can do better than that."

"Chloe."

Her laughter faded as she saw how serious he was. "You're kidding."

Luke shook his head. "I'm not." He looked so calm as he said it, as if they weren't discussing anything out of the ordinary.

She narrowed her eyes and scrutinized him. "And you know that because..."

"I work for the CIA too."

Chloe leaned back. This was insane. She fixed her eyes on him, half expecting him to start laughing, but there was nothing funny about his expression. "I was beginning to think you were a drug dealer or a mob hit man."

Dismay flared in his eyes. "Why does everyone always imagine the worst?"

Chloe was stunned into silence.

"Chloe, you know me."

"I thought I did, but…" She sighed.

"I met your aunt on an op. She had expertise in, among other things, abstract expressionism, which made her very useful back in the day. During the Cold War, the CIA sponsored abstract expressionism as a form of propaganda tool against the Russians."

"That's crazy."

He chuckled. "Oh, that's just the tip of the CIA-crazy iceberg, believe me." He leaned his elbow on the back of the sofa. "She was known in some circles as an art dealer."

"An art dealer?"

"It was a cover. Her work was all art related."

"I don't understand. Why?"

"That's all I can tell you except that she was good at her job. Shortly before she retired, she found this place, but she didn't like having neighbors so close. We were chatting one day. I'd been looking for a kind of getaway, and she told me about this neighborhood. The houses were both up for sale—some sort of family compound—

so we became neighbors. We looked out for each other."
He thought for a moment then spoke quietly. "I found
her when she died."

Chloe couldn't speak.

"I've wanted to tell you the truth—about both of
us." He exhaled, appearing dismayed. "A mob hit
man?"

Chloe shrugged. "Honest people don't have to hide
things."

"If I've withheld the truth, it's because I had to."

Questions swam about in her head in no logical
order. "You found my aunt?"

He nodded. "It was one of those perfect autumn
days, clear and sunny. The leaves were awash with
color. I looked over, and there she was in her studio,
painting. She once told me she was her happiest when
she was painting in that studio. Later, when I passed by
my window and looked over at her, she was on the floor.
When I got to her, she was gone."

Chloe stared into the fire. "Years ago, she told us to
stop contacting her."

Luke nodded. "There was an op that went bad. She
was compromised. She was determined to keep her
family safe, so she kept you in the safest place you could
be, out of her life."

"She must have been lonely."

"It gets like that sometimes. With no apparent
career, just a low-level government job, people view you
as an underachiever." He lifted an eyebrow. "Or a
crook. You can't tell them the truth. Questions come up

that you can't answer. Sometimes there's a personal cost."

Chloe met his gaze and felt every bit of guilt he must have wanted her to feel. "I'm sorry, but how was I to know?"

"I don't blame you. It's just one of those things that comes with the job. It's hard to have a normal social life."

"So this has happened before, with other women?"

"Yeah, but I've never told anyone—until you."

Chloe wanted to think that made her special to him, but she knew that wasn't the case. He'd only told her because she had stormed in and demanded an explanation. That didn't mean she was special. Even so, at least he had told her. She could feel safer now with him.

Luke leaned closer. "You cannot tell a soul."

"My mother needs to know."

"No." Luke stared into the fire. "It was a long time ago, but there are still relationships built on your aunt's work. It's like a game of Jenga. Each piece might seem innocuous enough, but you never know which bit of information could start the whole thing tumbling down. Don't tell her. Just leave it alone."

"Okay." Her head was spinning too much to argue. She reloaded the backpack. "Thank you for telling me."

She stood up, so Luke followed suit. He looked at her with concern. "Don't go."

"It's a lot to absorb. I need some time to sort through it." Part of her wanted to stay and talk or just be with him. She knew there must be more he could tell her about her aunt—little things, memories he might recall —but she couldn't do it right then. He didn't push. She was thankful for that.

Luke followed her to the door. "I'll watch until you're safely inside."

Chloe reached her front door and looked back to see him closing his door as she closed hers.

CHAPTER SIXTEEN

CHLOE COULDN'T PAINT. She'd barely slept. She couldn't think of anything but her aunt, the lost years without family. And she thought of Luke.

She looked around at her Christmas decorations. Behind all of the festive decorations was a house filled with secrets. She should have been satisfied knowing what Luke had told her, but now she wanted it all. If there was anything else in the attic, she needed to know. There were things Luke might not know, things that might explain who her aunt was and why she had chosen the life she'd lived.

Chloe climbed the attic stairs to sift through what was left. They wouldn't pertain to matters of national security, but Aunt Eleanor's boxes held clues to her personal life. One by one, Chloe went through the two dozen stacked boxes of old clothes and hats that had come back into style, some belts, and several pairs of shoes. It was an interesting lesson in fashion history, but it didn't tell her much about Aunt Eleanor.

In one box, old photographs lay in loose stacks. A few old albums were filled with black paper and photos held in place by black photo-mounting corners. In each photo, the faces of strangers looked out as the echoes of stories seemed to hover among them. Small items, collected and later neglected, revealed frozen moments in relationships that had long ago ended.

Chloe moved on to the hidden room, where her aunt's professional secrets had been hidden for years, undisturbed. A file cabinet held some old tax returns, her aunt's college diplomas, utility bills, and the deed to the house. That might have come in handy when her lawyer was trying to determine whether her aunt had possessed a clear title to the house, but it answered no questions about her aunt.

In the back of the drawer was a file marked "Family." Chloe pulled it out and opened it. On top lay a snapshot of their family in front of a Christmas tree. Even then, the family was small, consisting only of Chloe's grandparents, Chloe's parents, and Aunt Eleanor. Chloe studied her father closely. She'd never known him. He had died before she was born. She indulged in a moment to wonder what might have been if he'd lived. Then she looked at her mother, who looked about Chloe's current age. She and Aunt Eleanor were laughing. Chloe smiled and gently set it aside.

She came across a brown envelope and emptied its

contents. The first thing she picked up was a newspaper clipping about herself in her senior year of high
school when she'd won an art scholarship. The next was
a clipping of her beside one of her early paintings. She'd
won her first blue ribbon at that art show. The next
item was a school newspaper profile about her as an
incoming graduate student. Her work had caught a
good deal of attention that year. Chloe looked at her
face and saw all the career promise and hope that had
never panned out. The last item was Chloe's master's
thesis, "From Rivera to Banksy: Social Commentary in
Twentieth Century Murals and Street Art." Her aunt
had saved all of these clippings. She'd been following
Chloe's career.

Chloe set down the envelope and its contents. Aunt
Eleanor must have been disappointed to see Chloe's art
give way to a series of survival jobs in retail and food
service. All the potential she'd shown and six years of
university study had all come to that. Chloe smiled
through her tears. In leaving her estate to Chloe,
Eleanor had made it possible for her to follow her
dreams. Chloe looked about the room that was as secret
as her aunt's life.

Aunt Eleanor, I wish I'd been able to know you.

THE FOLLOWING DAY, Chloe's mother came over for
lunch. Chloe scanned the family Christmas photo she'd
found into her computer and gave the original to her

mother. Together they went to the cemetery and laid a wreath at Aunt Eleanor's grave.

Her mother said, "I remember her as always being there with us all but a little detached. She always seemed lost in thought, as if even while with us, she was living life elsewhere." She touched her hand to the gravestone. "But she loved us in her way. She was proud of you, Chloe."

She took Chloe's hand, and they walked to the car.

THEY HAD lunch at a crowded cafe in the middle of town. Inside, it was warm and inviting with carols softly playing through the overhead speakers. Twinkling Christmas lights were twisted around Mylar garland and fastened with bows on the walls.

Chloe warmed her hands on her coffee.

"So, you're neighbors. How close?"

"Across the street from each other." Chloe braced herself for what she knew from experience would be a series of questions.

"What did you say he does for a living?"

"I don't think I did. But he works for the government."

"Well that's good, steady work."

Chloe watched her mother's expression go from presumed disappointment that he wasn't a millionaire to relief that at least he wasn't an artist.

"And you've been going out for how long?"

"Mom, let's not get ahead of ourselves. We're just neighbors. We've been out a couple of times, but I wouldn't call them dates." *Except for the neighborly kissing.*

"Do you really think I can't read you? I don't blame you." She leaned forward as if she were telling a secret. "He's very attractive."

"Thanks, Mom. I hadn't noticed."

"But how much do you know about him?"

Chloe assumed the neutral stare she reserved for her mother at moments like this. "Enough."

Her mother lifted her eyebrows. "I hope so, for your sake."

"Ease up on the holiday cheer, Mom. Let's pace ourselves."

CHLOE PULLED into her driveway just as Luke was pulling out of his.

He rolled down his window. "I've been called in to work."

The news affected her more than she wanted to admit. "So you'll miss Christmas?"

"No, it's just a meeting. I'll be back later. I was wondering... Would you like to do something together when I get back? Or hang out here? I could stop and pick up a pizza on my way home." With amused reluctance, he said, "We could watch a Christmas movie."

How could she resist such an offer? "Okay. Sounds great!"

He looked so pleased that she couldn't help but return a broad smile. He winked. "I'll text you when I'm done."

"Okay." She waved as he drove off.

Chloe walked inside and made some coffee as if doing something so routine might make her feel like her life wasn't changing. But she felt like the ground was shifting beneath her, too little for anyone else to notice, but she couldn't quite keep her balance. Her heart was gone. Luke didn't know it yet, but it was his now. *Have I had any control of it since I met him?*

Her mother was right. Even now—especially now—that she knew what he really did for a living, there were so many reasons for caution. But when she was with Luke, nothing else mattered. She was under no illusions. The truth was, she didn't know where the relationship was going, but she didn't care as long as she was with him.

She thought about Luke all afternoon. She paced in her studio. There was so much that she didn't understand. She knew what she felt, but love was so much more than feelings. She stopped pacing. *Love.* That was what this was. Of course love had always been a possibility, but Chloe had always envisioned it as something in the future that she would see coming like a hazy mirage on the horizon, a promise that would slowly unfold, and yet might or might not turn out to be real.

She had never imagined that she would arrive there alone.

Does he feel it too? She had no idea and even less control. There was nothing she could do anymore. She just had to wait to find out whether the love she felt would fill her heart or break it. There seemed to be no in-between.

And that brought her back to the crux of her problem. Her heart might be out of control, but she still had a brain. If she couldn't control her feelings, at least she could determine her actions. Setting aside the issue of what Luke felt in return, there was the matter of his career. Every time he was called in to work, he wouldn't be able to tell her what he was doing or what sort of danger he was in. And he would be in danger. That much was certain. The guy had a bullet wound in his head for God's sake. *Is that something I can live with?*

She plopped down on an overstuffed chair by the window. *What am I doing, carrying on as though Luke even wants me in his life? Sure, we're great movie pals, but maybe I'm borrowing trouble. If I'm not, if he loves me and wants me in his life, what will I do?*

In that moment, she knew the answer. Despite all of her questions and doubts, she knew what she wanted —to spend her life with him. No matter what he did for a living or how frightened she was for his safety, she was willing to accept it because she loved him. She loved him no matter how many secrets he had to keep from her or how much danger he might face. She couldn't help loving him. She hoped he felt the same.

Dusk had fallen by the time Luke arrived home. He texted Chloe to say he would be there in a couple of minutes. Inside, he splashed water on his face and wiped it dry while he looked into the mirror. He combed his fingers through his hair, touching the scar that had become so familiar. He kept his hair a bit longer than was fashionable just to cover it. He'd grown so tired of people asking what had happened that he'd started telling them he'd fallen in a skateboard park. That always amused him. He'd never been on a skateboard in his life.

He walked into his bedroom and stared out the window. He could only see the shadowy outline of trees. He put on a clean shirt, donned his jacket, and headed over to Chloe's. They needed to talk.

Chloe opened her door with a smile, but it faded as soon as she looked at him. He hadn't meant to appear so serious, but she seemed to pick up on his mood none-theless.

Chloe poured him a glass of wine, and they sat by the fire. He'd spent so much of his life telling lies that he felt some relief to be able to let down his guard and honestly share how his meeting had gone. "The results came back from some medical tests."

Chloe fixed her eyes on his with quiet concern.

"I'm okay—fit to go back to work."

"And the headaches and threat of seizures?"

"There's nothing to indicate they'll recur."

Chloe nodded. "What comes next?"

"Back to work. I'll return after the holidays."

"That's good." She didn't look like she meant it, but he appreciated the effort.

"Yeah, it is."

"What would you have done if you hadn't been able to go back to work?"

"I thought about that. I'd change jobs. I could try to do something with my law degree. I knew a guy who worked for a government agency as a lawyer. From there, I could become an administrative law judge."

"Wait. Back up. Law degree?" Of all the things he had told her, this appeared to surprise her the most.

"Yeah, I'm a licensed attorney. I guess that's never come up. That's where I was recruited—in law school."

Chloe's eyebrows drew together. "So... men in black suits and aviator sunglasses just walked into class and handpicked you like they were choosing a team in PE?"

Luke laughed. "Not quite, but they were surprisingly open about it. It was listed just like the other jobs in the placement office."

Chloe stared in disbelief. "What, like 'Spy Wanted'?"

He grinned. "No, not exactly. It basically listed the agency and some sort of vague paragraph about what they were looking for. You know, there are a lot of jobs in the CIA besides spying."

Chloe stared off thoughtfully. "I guess there would be. I've never really thought about it."

"By my second year of law school, I knew I would hate being a lawyer, so I applied."

"Do you regret it?"

"No. I didn't exactly enjoy living a lie, but I believed in what I was doing. You learn to compartmentalize. I've tried to be honest, as much as I could, in my personal life." He took hold of her hand. "I've tried to be honest with you."

Chloe stared at their entwined hands. "I know." She looked a bit lost, as if she believed in him but wasn't yet comfortable with it. He couldn't blame her. Dating a spy wasn't anything she'd ever sought out, so he knew he couldn't be what she'd always wanted. He could only hope she would grow accustomed to the idea of dating someone in the CIA.

Chloe ran her fingers through her hair. "What's going to happen?"

"To us or to me... with my job?"

"Any of it. All of it. There are so many what-ifs."

"Why don't we just worry about us?"

She searched his eyes. "Us? I'm not sure what that is or what we can be."

"We're together. At least that's what I want us to be."

Chloe nodded with that same lost look in her eyes. "Me too. But there are so many unknowns."

Luke took her face in his hands. "Let's not worry about that now. Let's just take it one step at a time. Step one: we're together." He kissed her and enfolded her in his arms.

CHAPTER SEVENTEEN

DETERMINED to block out the world and its woes, Luke and Chloe set about enjoying the evening with a vengeance.

An hour into the evening, Chloe cried out in mock terror. "We've run out of wine!"

"Calm yourself, milady, I am always prepared. Let us go anon to my secret stash in yonder lair!"

Her eyes lit up. "So you've got a bottle stashed in your pantry? Awesome!"

He smiled. "Exactly! Let's go!"

They both threw on their boots and coats without bothering to zip them closed and ran out into the cold night. They crossed the road to Luke's house while laughing and kicking up snow in their wake. Luke unlocked the door while Chloe rubbed her bare hands and stomped her feet, then they hurried inside.

"How long does it take to get hypothermia?" she asked.

"At least fourteen minutes more than you spent out there in the cold. Sorry, but you'll have to go back outside and try harder. Although..." He drew her into his arms. "If you're worried about it, I can lend you some body heat." He kissed her and held her against him, which warmed them both up. Then he held her face and kissed her again. "Why did we come over here anyway?"

She laughed. "Wine!"

"Did I say I had wine?"

She opened her mouth to answer, but he kissed her before she could say anything.

His phone rang. He looked at it then wrinkled his face. He gave Chloe a helpless "I've got to take this" look. "Mom?"

"Are you still coming for Christmas? I know how you are," his mother said. She had every reason to doubt. He had canceled or been late for family Christmas dinners more often than not.

"Don't worry. I'll be there." While he chatted with his mother, he took Chloe's hand and led her to the pantry. He pulled a bottle of wine from the built-in wine rack and handed it to her along with a corkscrew he retrieved from a drawer. Chloe opened the bottle, found two glasses, and poured. She sat at the counter and sipped on her wine until he ended the call.

"Sorry. I was supposed to call home earlier, but I got distracted." He brightened his tone. "But we're not going to think about that tonight, are we?"

"No. We're going to go do something fun. What'll it

be? Frozen dinner and dancing? A movie?" She stopped and stared. On the floor, propped against one of the walls was a painting. "That's mine."

"I know." He'd meant to hang it before he let her see it.

"You bought it?"

"Well, I didn't steal it. Remember? I'm not a crook after all."

"I would have given you one."

He shrugged. "I wanted this one."

"That was really nice of you, but it feels like a pity purchase."

"What are you talking about? I saw it. I loved it. I bought it. Isn't that how it works, or am I missing something?"

"Thank you." She looked away, but he could tell she was bothered.

"Have I done something wrong?"

"No. But how would you feel if I sent you a check for clearing my driveway?"

"I don't know. I guess I'd feel like a professional driveway clearer." She wasn't amused. "Come on. The two aren't exactly comparable, are they? One is a purchase in a retail shop, and the other is a neighborly act."

"I guess." She heaved a sigh. "Thank you for buying my painting. I'm flattered—and richer. But next time, pay me in dinner or wine. Okay?"

He reached out and shook her hand. "Deal." Then he drew her closer and kissed her.

They decided to look for a movie to stream. While Luke scrolled through their options, Chloe asked, "What's your family like? You haven't told me anything about them."

"Okay, well, I've got two parents—the original set—and a brother. He works for a big investment firm and makes boatloads of money. They're very proud. And their other son... Well, I make a lot less. I think they envision me as a pocket-protector-clad pencil pusher for the State Department. I am their unfortunate under-achiever with two very expensive degrees. But I've managed to lower the bar enough that they now seem grateful I don't have masking tape holding my glasses together. In spite of it all, they love me and barely mention their disappointment anymore." He smiled. "I'm kidding. Sort of. They're actually very kind about it. And it's not that I couldn't tell them the truth. I'm allowed. But they'd worry. I don't want to put them through that. So this works well enough."

Chloe gazed at him. "For what it's worth, I thought you were amazing from the first—no, second—no, third time I saw you."

Luke leaned back. "First and second impressions were that bad?"

"Well, you've got to admit you're a little aloof."

"Occupational hazard."

"And I got the whole Christmas lights problem, but you said you hated Christmas carols. It was kind of a deal breaker."

Luke thought for a moment. "I'm not gonna lie. The ones that don't suck just don't get enough airplay."

Chloe winced. "Yeah, you've made your stance on that clear. I've reclassified it from deal breaker to something I'm still working through."

He looked at her dryly. "Keep me posted on your progress."

She pointed at the TV. "Stop! That's my favorite!"

Luke had been intermittently scrolling through movies. Maybe he should have scrolled faster. He winced. "*Love Actually*?"

Chloe clapped her hands together. "Yes! Let's watch that!"

All he could think of was how he should have searched by genre and avoided holiday movies altogether.

She laughed. "In college, my suitemates and I used to get up and dance with Hugh Grant in that scene. I can teach you the moves."

"No. I draw the line there—red line. No dancing."

Chloe nudged him with her shoulder. "Oh, c'mon!"

He raised an eyebrow.

"Okay, no dancing. But you've got to watch one Christmas movie."

Saying no when she had such holiday stars in her eyes would be cruel, so he exhaled, defeated. Chloe slipped her arm into his and snuggled closer. He was beginning to see a plus side to Christmas movies after all.

LUKE HAD MANAGED to ignore his career situation for the evening, but morning brought him back to nagging job uncertainty. He had told her only part of the job situation. He'd been consulting on an undercover assignment that looked as though it might take him out of the country for weeks. If those weeks turned to months, where that would leave things with Chloe was anyone's guess.

When she called and suggested they go into town, he was ready for a distraction. She giddily mentioned the annual Santa sleigh ride through town. She was way too in touch with her inner seven-year-old, yet that was one of the things about her he found most appealing. She had an open enthusiasm that was, even for him, contagious. He didn't even put up a fight. They got into the car and headed for town.

Hot chocolates in hand, they worked their way to Main Street, where they found Laura outside her shop. Her recessed doorway gave them a perfect viewing spot, so they stayed there and waited for Santa.

After a couple of minutes, Luke asked, "So when does the big parade start?"

Laura's eyes twinkled. "Don't get your hopes up. It's a small town and an even smaller parade. It's not even a parade, really. Just Santa. This is solely for the children. Local merchants go in on the candy. It's rumored that the local dentist pays more than his share. It's an investment."

"Look at the kids," Chloe exclaimed. "They're so happy!"

Laura went on to explain, "I shouldn't spoil the surprise for you, but there's just the one float. Santa's sleigh doesn't do well on salted, cleared roads, so one of the local farmers pulls a hay wagon with Santa's sleigh on top. And then there are the elves. A half dozen soccer moms dress up as elves and ride along, tossing candy to the children."

Luke turned to Chloe. "You're not going to line up with the kids, are you?"

"Don't tempt me. I mean, I could totally elbow those kids out of the way, but then I'd have to contend with their parents. I could take on the dads, but angry moms fight to the death."

Luke hooked his arm about Chloe. "That's what I love about you—kind and gentle, good to children and puppies." He gave her a kiss on the forehead.

A woman rushed up to Laura. "Santa's got the flu. He was determined to show up, and he did. But... well, let's just say it's a good thing we've got a spare Santa costume." She made a sour face that said it all.

Laura looked stricken with panic. "We don't have a Santa?"

She and the other woman tossed about names, but they had no idea where any of the potential Santas were in the crowd or if they were even there. Chloe looked crestfallen. The three women stared at each other, then as if on some cruel cue, they all turned and looked at Luke with raised eyebrows.

His eyebrows, in contrast, drew together. "No."

"You don't have to do anything," Laura said. "The elves do it all. You just sit there and wave—and say, 'Ho, ho, ho,' obviously."

Luke shook his head and held up his palms toward the women in protest.

Five minutes later, someone had tossed a Santa suit into his arms, and he was wondering how he had let himself get into such a predicament. One of the key requirements of his job was to keep a low profile—no traffic tickets, no public demonstrations, and nothing that might draw media attention. Implicit in that was no parading through town on Christmas Eve dressed as Santa. But thinking he was just painfully shy, the women all convinced him that he would be in disguise, so no one would ever know.

"Look at this beard," Chloe said. "In this, you are Santa—if Santa worked out, went meatless, and had Botox injections."

Luke gave her a wry look, but it only made Chloe smile more. She was enjoying the whole situation a little too much.

"I'll text everyone that we're ready to go," Laura said, reaching into her pocket. "Oh, man. My phone's gone."

The other woman held up her phone. "I got it." She sent a quick text then put her phone back in her purse. "Wait a minute. My wallet's gone."

"Pickpockets?" Chloe asked. "I've had people try when I travel, but I wouldn't expect it here."

"I'll text the police to be on the lookout," Laura's friend said.

Chloe was furious. "I can't believe people would do this on Christmas Eve."

Luke shrugged. "Crooks don't take a holiday."

She glared. "Nobody should steal on Christmas. The losers."

"Showtime." Laura swept her arm toward the sleigh. Luke sighed and climbed up into it.

As Santa's sleigh headed down Main Street, he looked down at the children's faces. He didn't spend much time with children, and he gave them even less thought. But as he looked at them lining the street with such innocent joy on their faces, his heart grew three sizes. They were just so darn cute, and they loved Santa so much. He was not going to admit it, but he was actually having fun. Making children happy was not a bad way to spend a Christmas Eve morning.

As he waved at the children and watched them scramble for the candy the elves were tossing at them, he spied a face that didn't quite look right. After more than a decade of keenly observing people, spotting someone out of place was automatic. There was something about that guy. He was looking the wrong way. Instead of facing Santa's sleigh or the children, his eyes shifted about. A boy who couldn't have been any older than eight reached into a woman's purse, pulled out a wallet, and handed it off to the guy Luke was eyeing. The two were working their way through the crowd.

Santa leapt from the sleigh and landed in a pile of

snow at the curb. Seeing this, the guy took off at a run, pushing onlookers out of the way. Santa's sleigh kept on going without him while Santa chased the pickpocket for two blocks, finally tackling him and knocking him to the ground. He pinned the guy down and held him until a police officer arrived and cuffed the crook.

Another officer arrived with the boy, who had taken off in the opposite direction. She said, "Look what I've found." She kept a firm grip on the child while she nodded at his backpack. "Santa, would you mind taking a look in there for me? My hands are full."

Luke took the boy's backpack and opened it up to reveal a lovely assortment of cell phones and wallets.

The officer gave the boy a stern look. "Come with me. We need to talk."

While the police escorted their suspects for the one-block walk to the station, Luke faded into the crowd, shedding his Santa costume as he went. He had already lost his white beard and hat.

After he tossed his red jacket to the ground, a young child came along and saw it. "Mommy, Santa melted!"

The mother said, "No, honey. He... wears layers. His jacket... probably just fell out of his sleigh."

Luke grinned and stepped behind some shrubs, shed the Santa pants he'd been wearing over his jeans, and crossed the street. He then doubled back toward Laura's.

"Luke?" Chloe found him pulling on his warm jacket.

"I need to speak with Laura and her friend." He took Chloe's hand, and they headed to Laura's store. When they met up with her and her friend, he made them promise not to tell anyone who Santa was.

Chloe looked on, stunned, as he convincingly lied and said he suffered from excruciating shyness. He told them that any attention he got over his Santa heroics would set him back six months or more from the progress he'd made in therapy. He was so good, Chloe began to feel sorry for him. That troubled her most of all. Lying seemed to come so easily to him.

Over lunch, Chloe studied Luke. "I've got this impression of you, but there's so much I don't know. Am I just seeing what I want to?"

Luke looked into her eyes. "I hope you see who I am. That's who I want you to see."

Chloe nodded, but she felt overwhelmed. "I just need to get used to this other side of you."

He reached across the table and put his hand on hers. "There's no pressure or hurry. I'm not going anywhere."

She squeezed his hand. "I'm not either."

CHAPTER EIGHTEEN

CHLOE FASTENED an earring and answered the door with a broad smile, then she got her coat from the closet. "You're early. Can't wait to get to the Christmas Eve service? It's the carol singing, isn't it?" She turned and froze.

Luke held out his phone to her. Something was wrong.

It took her a moment to realize what she was looking at. On his phone was a social media photo of him in the Santa suit, glancing up as he held down the pickpocket and looked for police. His hat and beard had come off in the struggle. She looked at Luke with alarm.

"I'm trending on social media," he said, looking stunned.

Chloe did a quick search on the phone's browser. The story had been picked up by some media outlets as well. She read some of the headlines out loud. "Santa Pummels Pickpocket. Santa Claus is Coming with

Cuffs. He Sees You When You're Stealing." Finally, she turned off the phone and handed it back.

Luke took the phone and shook his head slowly. "I've got to disappear before the media finds me. If it gets out who I really am, my house will be swarming with reporters and photographers. They'll come here to your house, asking questions. You should go stay with your mother." He put his hands on her shoulders. "Do not talk to anyone, no matter what."

He was scaring her. "Where are you going?"

"I don't know. I'll get in touch when I can."

"When?"

His eyes fixed on hers. "It might be a while."

She searched his eyes as questions flashed in her mind, but she wouldn't trouble him.

He gazed intently. "Pack and leave as soon as you can—in ten minutes, fifteen tops. Plan to be gone for a few days at least, maybe a week. I'm not sure what's going to happen with work. If I'm not back right away, tell anyone who asks that we broke up."

"What?"

"It'll keep them from asking more questions." He clutched her against him for too brief a moment and kissed her. "I've got to go." He kissed her again as if he were saying goodbye forever. "Don't worry." Then he left.

Chloe's hands shook as she packed a suitcase and tossed it, along with a shopping bag full of presents, into her trunk. As she drove down the mountain, she passed a car, then another. Reporters already?

She hadn't even wished Luke a Merry Christmas.

CHLOE SPENT a melancholy Christmas with her mother then rang in the New Year trying not to worry about Luke. On New Year's Day, she went home. The reporters were gone. No one cared about Santa since Christmas was over. Her mailbox was full of junk mail, but there was nothing from Luke. She obsessively checked her email and voice mail for days. A month passed with no word. She clung to the memory of his last kiss and embrace and reminded herself that he'd warned her he might be gone long.

As she did every week, she made a routine trip into town and stopped by Laura's shop to say hello and to check on how her paintings were selling.

She did as Luke had suggested and told people they'd broken up. She hated the lie, but she couldn't deny that, for the most part, it made things easier for her. No one asked about him anymore, and most didn't even ask about her. But, in one way, it made everything worse because she was left with no one to talk to about Luke. He became a sad, lonely ache in her heart, so much so that she began to believe it might really be over between them.

Laura greeted her warmly, as always. Her friend may not have known the truth about Chloe and Luke, but she knew that Chloe was hurting. They'd talked about it a couple of times until Chloe had finally said it was too hard to talk about anymore. At least that part was true. If she couldn't talk about the truth, there was no point in talking at all.

Laura's face brightened. "Oh, someone stopped by two days ago. He took an interest in your work, but he said he really preferred abstract expressionism."

That piqued Chloe's interest, and her face must have shown it. "That's not even close to my work."

"I know. I explained that we don't really sell much of that. Our clientele tends to like realism along the lines of Wyeth, Hopper, that sort of thing. He didn't look too surprised. But he really spent time looking at your paintings. I was sure he was going to buy one, but he just gave me his card and said to call him if I got any abstract expressionism in."

"May I see the card?"

"Sure." Laura looked under the counter. "Here it is."

Chloe tried not to show how fast her heart was pounding. "May I take a picture of it?"

"Sure."

"What did he look like?" she asked as she snapped a photo of the card.

Laura thought for a moment, slowly shaking her head. "Average height, thinning hair, glasses."

Chloe glanced at her watch. "Oh, wow. I've lost track of the time. I've still got shopping to do, and I need to get home for a one o'clock business call."

A customer arrived at the counter with a handful of items.

"I'll let you go," Chloe said. "Good to see you!"

She couldn't walk quickly enough to her car. Someone named Leonard Anderson—the same initials as Luke—had asked about abstract expressionist paintings by Chloe? No one would have looked at her paintings and even thought that, let alone asked if she had anything like it. So for someone with Luke's initials to make such an inquiry was too coincidental. It had to have something to do with Luke. She didn't recognize the man's description, but Luke must have sent him. The details were just too specific.

She got into her car, locked the door, and immediately pulled out her phone. She dialed *67 to block the caller ID, just in case it turned out to be some dogged reporter who'd tracked her down and been lucky enough to mention the painting style that her aunt had known so well. She dialed the number on the card. While it rang, she glanced around, her pulse racing. When she heard the tone and a recorded voice, she stopped and stared at her phone. *Disconnected?* She leaned her head back on the headrest. *How could it be disconnected?* She tried again, but the result was the same. She took in a deep breath and exhaled. *Luke, what does it mean?*

While she drove home, she mulled everything over. Other than studying it in art school, the only connection Chloe had to the abstract expressionist movement was through her aunt, and the only person who knew that was Luke. But why would he torment her by leaving a disconnected phone number? Unless he'd never intended to speak with her directly. Or maybe he couldn't. It could simply have been a way to make contact, to let her know he was safe and that he was thinking of her. But why couldn't he come himself? *Where is he?* At least he'd found a way to make contact. That was something. But it wasn't enough.

If there was any other explanation, Chloe couldn't come up with one, so she chose to assume Luke was sending a message. But she still didn't understand why he would send it via the mysterious man in the shop. More importantly, she hoped she was understanding him fully and there wasn't a coded message she'd missed.

Her heart sank at the thought that she'd overlooked something vital. But he had to expect that she might not be able to decipher a code. She forced herself to stop trying to see what wasn't there. Luke knew her. She trusted that any message he tried to convey would be clear. The most obvious message must have been that he was okay.

She missed Luke and worried about him, but there was nothing she could do. She redirected her energy into something she could control, her art. The more she missed Luke, the more she immersed herself in her painting and business. Learning as she went along, she was steadily building a business, and the progress was satisfying. She was enjoying her life as an artist.

Two weeks after the shop visit, a postcard arrived. On it was a common Forever flag stamp, and it was post-marked Washington, DC, but nothing was written on it except her address. On the other side of the card was a Mark Rothko painting. There was no meaningful clue in the painting that she could discern, but the artist himself was a clue. Rothko was an abstract expressionist. She turned the card over again and looked at the small print. "National Gallery of Art, Washington, DC." The CIA headquarters was in the DC area. Maybe Luke was there but unable to reach her. Or maybe he was somewhere else, on a covert op, and someone—perhaps the man in the shop—was mailing the postcard to her. Part of her found that idea too cloak-and-dagger to believe, yet it was the only potential connection she had to Luke, so she clung to her theory.

As the dreary weeks of winter wore on, more blank Rothko postcards came postmarked from various locations in the DC area. Every two weeks another would appear in her mailbox, renewing her hope. Luke was out there somewhere, letting her know he was thinking of her and that he was okay.

CHAPTER NINETEEN

April arrived, and signs of new growth on the plants and trees lifted Chloe's spirits. Her online business was flourishing, keeping her busy—almost busy enough to distract her from Luke. One morning, she pulled into the post office parking lot for what had become an almost daily routine of shipping artwork and related merchandise to customers. As she arrived at the entrance, the door swung open, and she collided with the man coming out, sending her packages to the ground.

He touched her shoulders to steady them both. "Chloe?"

She looked up, surprised. "Easton! Hello!"

He stooped down to retrieve the fallen boxes. "Here, let me help you." When they'd gathered them up, Easton carried the boxes inside. He waited while Chloe finished, then said, "Would you like a coffee?"

Coffee sounded like an excellent idea on its own,

and coffee with Easton would be even better. "Yes. Coffee sounds good."

The post office was two blocks away from the deli with the best coffee in town, so they walked there. As Chloe walked in, she glanced at the table where she'd once sat with Luke. It seemed like a lifetime ago.

"After you." Easton was waiting.

Only then did Chloe realize she had stopped. "Sorry." She continued to the counter, where they got two coffees then made their way to a table.

Easton smiled, flashing bright eyes and those perfect white teeth of his. "It is so good to see you."

"You too." Not only did she mean that sincerely, but she felt more alive than she'd felt in some time—well, since she'd last seen Luke. A pang of guilt brought her back to reality. She was lonely. That's what this was about. And Easton was here looking very attentive.

They chatted mostly about Chloe. Easton was far too skilled at asking questions and even better at listening to the answers. Chloe talked about her painting and how her business was growing.

"I'm not surprised. I knew you would do well."

With a light laugh, Chloe said, "That makes one of us."

When they'd caught up and arrived at a lull in the conversation, Easton gazed at her. "I'm so glad I ran into you—literally."

"Me too." She meant it more than she cared to admit. As much as she cared for Luke, she didn't know where he was, when she'd see him again—if ever—or whether he would still feel the same about her. What she had with Luke was more mirage than relationship, but her heart would not let go.

Easton glanced at his watch and looked at her with reluctance. "I've got to go to a meeting."

Chloe smiled, feeling glad she had seen him but relieved to be parting.

His eyebrows drew together. "Would you like to go out sometime?"

She was tempted. "I'm seeing someone."

Easton looked genuinely pleased for her. "Lucky him."

"I don't know about that." She peered into his eyes. "It was so good to see you."

They got up, went outside, and hugged outside the door before parting. As she walked to her car, Chloe thought about Easton. As nice as his company was, it could only come close to what she had with Luke. As lonely as she might feel at times, her heart was with Luke.

Months passed, and the postcards piled up in a wooden box on Chloe's counter. She kept them there, where she could look at them often. But as the seasons changed and she spent day after day alone, she began to feel as though she had fallen in love with a ghost. Regardless of that, she *had* fallen in love.

Sometimes she would look at Luke's house and imagine him there like he used to be. A crew came by every week and maintained the lawn. When the first snow came in November, the driveway was plowed.

Lights came on and off with a timer, making it almost appear as if someone were living there. Thanksgiving came and went, and Chloe didn't have the heart to put up her usual Christmas decorations. Every time she thought about stringing up lights, her thoughts went to Luke, and she couldn't do it. She'd lost her Christmas spirit.

Her mother took her out for some Christmas shopping and lunch. "Chloe, maybe it's time to let go."

Chloe didn't say anything. If she were her mother, she would say the same thing. It had been nearly a year since she'd met Luke, and most of that year, she had spent all alone. While the Santa photo may have outed him to a certain extent, no one had ever connected him to the CIA. If they had, the media would have been all over it. Time had passed. No one seemed to remember or care about the small-town Santa story. Luke was gone. Life went on.

Chloe went home from lunch and checked her mailbox. Her Rothko postcard was several days late. Maybe her mother was right. Maybe Luke had decided it was time for them both to let go. Chloe put on her comfy pants, started her "Sad Christmas" playlist, and sat by the fireplace, nursing a hot chocolate laced with her teardrops.

Two days before Christmas, the mail truck pulled away, and she went to the mailbox again. Still no Rothko postcard. If it hadn't come by that point, it wasn't coming at all. She was sifting through junk mail, quickly tossing items into the trash, when she came across a mailer from a church in New York. It was a photo of their men and boys' choir with the Fifth Avenue church's beautiful sanctuary as a backdrop. She would have been all over that sort of thing in years past, but this Christmas was different. Besides, it was too far away. In fact, for that reason, it seemed odd that they would have bothered to send her a mailer. She'd never visited the church or signed up for their mailing list.

She examined it further. It hadn't been sent via bulk mail. It bore the same flag stamp as the Rothko postcards. But that didn't mean anything. That stamp had to be the most common stamp in use. Then she noticed the postmark—Washington, DC. Why would a church in New York City send her a postcard from Washington, DC?

Because they haven't. At least she didn't think so. She couldn't be sure, but she thought Luke might have sent it. Every other card he'd sent had been from that same Rothko set of postcards. They'd held no clue of a time or place, but this one was different. It still had no message—only her address, the flag stamp, and the DC postmark—but it advertised an event, the Christmas Eve midnight service. It couldn't be a coincidence.

She reached for her phone. "Mom? I'm going to New York for Christmas Eve. I'll be back Christmas Day."

"New York? Why?"

"I'm not sure. I'll explain later."

"But Chloe—"

"I'll be fine. I'm not driving. I'm taking a train from Harrisburg."

"But that'll take hours."

"Four. Yes, I know."

The next afternoon, she was on the train, staring out the window at the passing scenery and wondering if she'd lost her mind. She arrived in New York and checked into a hotel. With a few hours to spare before the midnight Christmas Eve service, Chloe was tired but too nervous to nap, so she went for a walk. After taking in the store window displays, she turned down a side street. Drawn in by its twinkling holiday lights, she ducked into an Irish pub for some dinner. After returning to her hotel, Chloe freshened up then found herself with thirty minutes to spare. She went down to the hotel bar, which was practically empty. There, she sat in a quiet corner and calmed her nerves with a brandy eggnog. Her mind swam with conflicting thoughts. Maybe the mailer was just Luke saying Merry Christmas—a simple thought that she'd taken and run way too far with. But what if it was more than that? She had to know.

CHAPTER TWENTY

SHE ARRIVED at the church early, but a line was already forming. She kept looking for Luke, but he wasn't there. She told herself it was early. The doors opened, and Chloe found a seat about halfway back on the aisle. She watched as people filed in. The church filled up quickly, but she kept her coat beside her and vigilantly guarded the extra space on the pew.

The service began, and Chloe's heart sank. She'd known he might not be there, but she had let herself hope. The choir sang "In the Bleak Midwinter," and the beauty of their singing made Chloe feel just as bleak. Everyone seemed to be there with someone, but she was alone on Christmas Eve. She blocked out her disappointment until she felt almost numb. A boy's pure solo soprano began, "Once in Royal David's City." The exquisite clarity of his voice and the deep meaning of Christmas mingled with her profound disappointment. A tear trailed down her cheek.

A latecomer arrived and stood in the aisle beside her. There was no point in saving the seat anymore, so she moved her coat onto her lap to make room on the pew. She glanced up out of reflexive politeness to offer a nod, but she couldn't manage a smile.

Luke looked into her eyes. Everyone stood to sing "O Come All Ye Faithful," and she numbly stood along with them. Luke leaned over and said, "It's over. I've come back to you—if you still want me." He slipped his arm about Chloe's waist, and she sank against him.

She sang one line of a verse then whispered, "I've missed you." She stopped talking as tears unexpectedly filled her eyes.

He didn't answer, but his aching gaze said it all.

The initial wonder and joy of being together subsided, and they couldn't seem to stop smiling. By the last verse, Chloe whispered, "I thought you couldn't sing."

"I never said that. I'll have you know I was the section leader in my high school choir."

"But you hate Christmas carols."

"Not the good ones. I just hate what you hear in the mall."

"I've got to know. Who was the man in Laura's shop?"

"One of my coworkers." He shrugged as though it were nothing, but that question had nagged her for months.

"He sent the cards?"

Luke nodded. "I left him a box of them before I left."

She opened her mouth to say something more, but he held up his finger to shush her and glanced toward the altar to remind her that they were in church. Then his eyes twinkled.

Luke slipped his hand in hers and held it until the music was over. Then he leaned over and whispered, "I love you."

"I love you too. I've been wanting to say that for so long."

As glorious voices filled the church, Chloe sat beside Luke, overwhelmed by the joy of both Christmas and Luke's return. She didn't know where he had been, and she might never know. The fact that he was even there with her was a gift on its own. The world wasn't perfect, but there were unsung heroes like Luke who were making it safer. Meanwhile, inside where it was safe and warm, she had someone beside her to share Christmas and love, and that was a gift she would treasure forever.

CHAPTER TWENTY-ONE

Four Months Later

Chloe sat at the computer in her studio and reread the ad copy. Luke came inside, all sweaty from yard work, and opened his arms. Chloe laughed and pulled away. "That's okay."

His eyes twinkled. "Honeymoon's over already?"

She tilted her head and narrowed her eyes. "Check back after you've showered, and I might reconsider."

"Oh, I will, and you'd better."

They shared a lingering look, then his eyes strayed to the computer screen.

"What do you think of this ad for your house vacation rental?"

Luke read it and smiled. "It's perfect."

Chloe pressed Enter and posted the ad.

. . .

THE HOLIDAY HIDEAWAY: *Escape to an enchanting mountaintop forest retreat. Rustic character meets modern, upscale amenities in this two-bedroom, two-bath cabin just waiting for you.*

THE HOLIDAY
HOUSE COLLECTION

Don't miss the remaining books in the Holiday House
Collection:
The Christmas Cabin
The Winter Lodge
The Lighthouse
The Christmas Castle
The Beach House
The Christmas Tree Inn
The Holiday Hideaway

THANK YOU!

Thank you for reading! If you enjoyed this book, please consider leaving a review or a rating. Your feedback on bookstore, Goodreads, and Bookbub websites helps other readers discover books they'll enjoy.

instagram.com/jljarvis.writer

facebook.com/jljarvis1writer

x.com/JLJarvis_writer

youtube.com/@jljarvis-author

goodreads.com/jljarvis

bookbub.com/authors/j-l-jarvis

ALSO BY J.L. JARVIS

Waterfront Summers

(Can be read in any order)

The Cottage at Peregrine Cove

The House on Serenity Lake

Moonlight on Mariner's Bluff

Drake & Wilde Mysteries

(Reading Order)

Love in the Time of Pumpkins

Secrets in the Hollow

Shadow of the Horseman

Standalones

(Can be read in any order)

A Cowboy Kind of Love

A Christmas Eve Stop

Christmas by Lamplight

A Kiss in the Rain

App-ily Ever After

Once Upon a Winter

The Red Rose

Highland Vow

Short Stories

(Can be read in any order)

The Magic of Snow

The Eleventh-Hour Pact

A Christmas Yarn

The Farmer and the Belle

Work-Crush Balance

Cedar Creek

(Can be read in any order)

Christmas at Cedar Creek

Snowstorm at Cedar Creek

Sunlight on Cedar Creek

Pine Harbor

(Reading Order)

Allison's Pine Harbor Summer

Evelyn's Pine Harbor Autumn

Lydia's Pine Harbor Christmas

Holiday House

(Can be read in any order)

The Christmas Cabin

The Winter Lodge

The Lighthouse

The Christmas Castle

The Beach House

The Christmas Tree Inn

The Holiday Hideaway

Highland Passage

(Can be read in any order)

Highland Passage

Knight Errant

Lost Bride

Highland Soldiers

(Reading Order)

The Enemy

The Betrayal

The Return

The Wanderer

American Hearts

(Can be read in any order)

Secret Hearts

Forbidden Hearts

Runaway Hearts

For more information, visit jljarvis.com.

Get monthly book news at news.jljarvis.com.

ABOUT THE AUTHOR

J.L. Jarvis is a left-handed former opera singer/teacher/lawyer who writes books. She now lives and writes on a mountaintop in upstate New York.

jljarvis.com